Neighborhood Watch

From the Tales of Dan Coast

Neighborhood Watch

From the Tales of Dan Coast

By

Rodney Riesel

Published by Island Holiday Publishing
East Greenbush, NY

Special thanks to:

Pamela Guerriere

Kevin Cook

Cover Image by:

Kim Seng at RoyalStockPhoto.com

Cover Design by:

Connie Fitsik

To learn about my other books friend me at

https://www.facebook.com/rodneyriesel

For Brenda,
Kayleigh, Ethan
& Peyton

Chapter One

The sun was just dipping into the horizon as Dan rounded the corner onto Beach View Street. He had taken the long way home and stopped at the Key West Cigar Club to pick up just the right cigar for a tequila, Seven, and lime by the fire pit. He chose a six-inch Camacho with a Maduro wrapper. He couldn't wait to get home, and lit it in the car before his drive.

Dan could see Maxine standing at the bottom of the steps as he approached his house. He felt a chill and the hair on his arms stood up. He pulled the Porsche into the driveway and shut off the engine.

"Hey," Maxine said.

"Hey," Dan replied. He got out of the car and took a long drag on the cigar.

"What's been going on?"

"Not much. Been kinda slow around here."

"What happened to the window?"

Dan glanced at the plywood he'd nailed over the broken window. "Kids," he replied.

"I thought you would be at Red's. I was just about to drive over there."

Dan moved a little closer. "No. I figured I would stay in tonight. Maybe sit by the fire and have a smoke."

"Oh."

Dan took another step closer. "Are you back?" he asked.

Maxine nodded her head. "Yes."

Dan took another puff on his stogie. He removed it from his mouth and gently peeled off the wrapper. "I mean, to stay?" he asked.

Dan dropped the cigar on the sidewalk, took Maxine's hand in his, and got down on one knee. He held the cigar wrapper between his fingers and stared up at the woman he loved. "It's horrible when you're not here."

Maxine's eyes widened.

"Maxine Meyers, will you marry me?"

Maxine stared down at her boyfriend. She began to tremble, and a tear formed in the corner of her eye. She placed her right hand on her stomach in an attempt to calm the butterflies. "You ... you mean, right now?"

"What?" Dan asked.

"What are you asking me?"

Dan looked confused. "I'm asking you to marry me."

"Oh."

"Well?"

"Well, what?"

"Are you going to marry me?"

"Well, eventually. I mean … I figured we would—"

"Are you turning me down? I'm confused."

"No, I'm not turning you down."

"So then, it's a yes?"

Maxine looked around the neighborhood, then up the street one way and down the other. She noticed Edna McGee staring out her front window. Old man Stein was standing on his front porch, rocking on his heels, thumbs tucked in his suspenders, avidly watching them. Young Julian Thompson whizzed past on his bicycle.

"Hi, Dan! Hi, Maxine!" Julian shouted from the street.

"Hey, Julian!" Dan hollered back, without looking.

Behind him, Dan heard a strange squeaking sound, like a hamster on a running wheel. He turned around to see the canary yellow box on wheels. The vehicle lurched to shaky stop, backfired, and lurched again. Skip Stoner sat behind the wheel of his convertible Volkswagen Thing; Red Baxter was in the passenger seat. The top was down.

"Dan the man!" Skip shouted. "Whatcha doin' on your knees?"

"What the Christ!" Dan shouted; he let go of Maxine's hand.

"What's up, pal?" Red asked.

"Oh, nuthin'," Dan responded sarcastically.

"Maxine, you're home," said Skip, stating the obvious.

"Yup," Maxine replied. "I'm home."

Red held up two six-packs of LandShark Lager, one in each hand. "Good, we can all celebrate together."

"Celebrate?" Maxine asked.

"You coming home," said Red. He stood in the seat and jumped over the door of the open convertible. His giant feet hit the ground with a thud, kicking up a cloud of dust.

"Awesome," Maxine responded.

Skip climbed out of his side and lumbered around to the sidewalk. "This is great," he said. "Having the whole crew back together again."

"Yeah, swell," Dan said.

Red and Skip walked up the driveway and down the gravel path that led to the two Adirondack chairs next to the fire pit.

Dan turned back to Maxine. He smiled. "I guess that means you're part of the crew now."

"I'm honored," Maxine responded.

"Sorry."

"About what?"

Dan waved his hands around. "This whole thing."

"It's okay. I wouldn't have it any other way." She leaned in and gave Dan a kiss on the lips.

"Shall we join them?" Dan asked.

"Sure."

Dan stepped back to let Maxine go first. As they walked down the path, Maxine said, "Yes."

"Yes what?" Dan asked.

"Really?" Maxine asked.

"Oh, you mean, *yes*."

"Yes."

"Okay then, that's settled."

"Yup. Let's celebrate."

When Dan and Maxine arrived at the fire pit Red had already gotten the extra lawn chairs out of the wood shed. Maxine took a seat in one of the Adirondack chairs; Red was seated in the other.

"You're in my seat," Dan said.

Red pointed at one of the lawn chairs. "I got you a lawn chair," he said.

"I want to sit in that chair," Dan complained.

Red raised his hands. "Sorry, pal. Possession is 9 percent of the law."

"Possession is nine-tenths of the law," Dan corrected.

"So we're in agreement," said Red. "Now sit in the damn lawn chair."

Dan sat down in the lawn chair. "You're a moron."

"A moron in a comfortable chair." Red grinned as he twisted the top off of a LandShark and handed it to Maxine.

"Thanks, Red," Maxine said.

Red twisted the top off a beer for himself. "What's that on your finger?" he asked, taking a big swig of his beer.

Maxine held out her hand and looked at the cigar band. Then she turned her head questioningly toward Dan.

Dan nodded his approval. "It's my engagement ring," she announced.

Red did a spit take. "What?" he hollered. He jerked his head around in the direction of his best friend.

Skip's eyes were going back and forth from Maxine to Dan like a dog watching a game of Frisbee.

"Is she serious?" Red asked.

"She is," said Dan.

Skip and Red both jumped out of their chairs.

"Holy crap, Dan the Man!" Skip yelled. He grabbed Dan by the arm and yanked him out of his chair. He threw his long, spindly arms around Dan, wrapping him in a big bear hug. "Congratulations!"

Maxine stood and Red hugged her. "This is so awesome," Red said. "I've never been a best man before."

"And I've never been in a wedding at all," said Skip.

When Dan finally broke free from Skip's grip, he noticed the tears running down the young man's face.

"Are you crying?" Dan asked.

"I always cry at weddings, dude" Skip replied.

"This isn't a wedding," Dan pointed out.

"I'll even be worse on that day," said Skip, wiping his eyes with the back of his hand.

Dan heard the distinctive creaking of the back screen door of his next-door neighbor, Bev. Bev and Dan's dog, Buddy, stepped out onto the deck. "What's all the shouting about," Bev asked.

"Dan and Maxine are gettin' hitched," Red shouted. "I'm gonna be a best man!"

"And I'm gonna be one of the other dudes," Skip shouted.

"Other dudes?" Dan asked.

"You know," Skip explained, "those usher dudes, or whatever."

"Oh, that's right," Dan said. "The ever-important usher dudes."

"Or groomsmen dudes, they're sometimes called," said Maxine.

It only took a few seconds for Bev to cross the yards and reach the group. She went to Maxine first and gave her a hug and a kiss on the cheek. "Congratulations, Maxine," she said. She turned to Dan and did the same. "We have a date set?"

"Not yet," Maxine replied.

Bev turned back to Maxine. "Let's see that ring."

Maxine held out her hand to reveal the cigar band that was wrapped around her ring finger. Bev shot Dan a look. "Really? A cigar band?"

"It was spur of the moment," Dan defended.

"I guess so," said Bev. "Someone better get to the jewelry store."

"You," Skip said, pointing at Dan.

"Yeah, Skip, I know she means me."

"Well, I guess at least this way you'll get to pick out the one you want," said Bev, "instead of whatever cheap ass ring he would have picked out."

Maxine laughed.

"How much do they say you're supposed to pay for a ring?" Red asked.

"Who are *they*?" Dan asked.

"The ring experts, I guess," Red replied. He sat back down in his seat, and everyone else did the same. Bev took Dan's chair, which left him standing.

"They say it should be around one month's salary," Skip offered.

"*They*," Dan repeated.

"One month's salary," Red said. "Let's see, that would be—wait a minute. Did you make any money this month?"

Dan thought for a second. "Nope," he said. "As a matter of fact, I'm a few grand in the hole due to the big expenditure from my last case."

"Well that settles it, Maxine," Bev said. "It looks like the cigar band was the exact price it was supposed to be."

"Actually," said Dan. "That cigar cost nine dollars, so it was a more than what *they* say it should cost."

"Well," Maxine said, "at least I didn't end up owing *him* money."

"We'll go to the jewelry store tomorrow," Dan said.

"You bet your sweet ass we will," Maxine responded.

"Can me and Red Man come?" Skip asked.

"No," Dan said.

"Why not?" Red protested.

"Because it has nothing to do with you."

"I beg to differ, brodiddly," said Skip.

"You can beg all you want," Dan said. "But you ain't coming with us."

"That's so bogus," Skip mumbled.

"Yeah, *really* bogus," Red added.

Dan dropped his empty beer bottle on the grass. "Toss me another one of those," he said.

Red pulled another bottle from the six-pack and tossed it to his friend. "You should light a fire," Red said. "It's cold."

"Cold?" Dan asked.

"It's almost seventy."

"That's what I said. It's cold."

Dan shook his head. "At home, if it was seventy, we would—"

"At home?" Maxine interrupted. "You are home, and it is chilly, so build a damn fire."

"Wow," Dan said. "Slip a cigar band on a woman's finger and she gets pretty damn bossy." He headed for the woodshed.

Maxine turned to Bev. "He ain't seen nothin' yet," she whispered. The two women burst out laughing.

Chapter Two

The following day Dan knelt on the couch, facing backwards. With his index finger he held the curtain open a few inches and stared out the window that overlooked the driveway and the house next door. Maxine was clearing the lunch dishes from the table. She paused with dishes in her hand and watched her nosy boyfriend.

"Who are you spying on?" Maxine asked.

"I'm not spying on anyone," Dan replied.

"What do you call what you're doing?"

"Keeping my neighborhood safe."

"Safe from who?"

"There's some lady moving in next door at the Stewart's place. She's only brought in two suitcases so far."

"And you're keeping the neighborhood safe from her?"

"Maybe. Why would someone rent a house for the week and only bring two suitcases?"

Maxine turned and went into the kitchen. "Does she appear threatening?" she called out.

Dan ignored the question.

When Maxine returned to the dining room she said, "I'm surprised you don't have your camera and binoculars out."

"Camera," Dan whispered to himself. He started to get off the couch.

"No," Maxine ordered. "You're not going to take pictures out the window every time a new vacationer rents the house next door."

Dan sighed. "Fine."

"You're just bored. Why don't you go see what Red or Skip are doing?"

"I thought you wanted to go to the jewelry store?"

"We can go later this afternoon."

"I don't know. Maybe—" Dan froze at the sound of a small metal door being slammed. "Mail's here!" he announced, and jumped from the couch and headed for the door.

"Yeah, you're just bored," said Maxine. She picked up the loaf of bread, spun the wrapper closed, and retied the twisty. She grabbed the two glasses in her other hand and returned to the kitchen.

Dan hurried down the steps to the mailbox that sat on a post at the end of his sidewalk. He yanked open the door and looked inside. There was a small package, a few bills, and some junk mail. Dan inspected each envelope and then noticed that the package wasn't for him. "640 Beach View

Street," he read to himself. "Hey!" he shouted down the street. "Hey! This package isn't mine!"

The mailman spoke on his cell phone as he walked along.

"Hey!" Dan shouted again. Still the mailman didn't hear him ... or pretended not to. "What the Christ?" Dan started jogging toward the carrier. As he ran past the neighbor's house he glanced at the car in the driveway: a green, older model BMW with Florida tags. The trunk was open, and inside was one more suitcase—smaller than the ones she had already brought in. Dan looked up at the front door of the house. A woman in her late forties or early fifties stood in the doorway. "Good morning," Dan said.

The stone-faced woman gave a slight nod of her head. Dan returned his attention to the postman.

When Dan reached the mailman, he said, "This isn't my package."

The mailman looked at Dan and then down at the package. "Hold on a second," he said into his cell phone, then turned back to Dan. "What's your problem, sir?" he said in a tone that indicated he didn't give a damn what Dan's problem was.

"My problem?" Dan asked. His eyebrows rose in twin peaks of annoyance. "My problem is *you*. You walk around the streets with that goddamn cell phone jammed in your head and then you stick shit in my mailbox that isn't mine ... like this package. Then I have to walk around the street and deliver my neighbor's mail to them. In a sense I'm doing your job, only I'm not getting paid for it."

"Whose is it?" asked the letter carrier indifferently. He scratched his greasy black hair triggering a snowstorm of dandruff on his shoulders. He looked at his fingernails and then wiped them on his pants.

"Well, ya see, Cliff Clavin," Dan explained. "If you look right here on this label, there's a number. Now your job, in case no one has ever explained it to you, is to match the number on the letter or package with the number on one of these mailboxes." Dan held the package out to the vacuous twenty-something.

The kid snatched the package. "I know what my job is, mister."

"Evidently you don't, because that number on that label and the number on my mailbox are not the same."

"Dan!" Maxine hollered. She was standing on the sidewalk in front of Dan's house with her arms folded and her hip pushed out. Dan ignored her.

"Sorry, sir" the kid said, suddenly contrite. "It was just an honest mistake."

"No," Dan replied. "The mistake was giving you this job instead of giving it to a chimp who is probably more qualified than you." Dan turned and stalked homeward. "And stay off your goddamn cell phone while you're working."

Maxine waited like an angry little statue until Dan reached her. "Picking on the mailman again?" she asked.

Dan walked past her and up the steps. "Someone's gotta teach that kid how to do his job."

"Yeah, yeah," said Maxine as she followed him into the house.

"When I was his age you wouldn't have caught me on my cell phone all day while I was supposed to be working."

"Did they even have cell phones when you were his age?"

"Very funny, Maxine." Dan tossed the mail onto the table. "Is there still coffee in that pot?"

"Yes. You want me to make a fresh pot?"

"No. I'll just nuke it."

Maxine opened one of the envelopes and pulled out a card. "Oh this will be fun," Maxine said.

"What will be fun?" Dan asked as he poured himself a cup of cold coffee.

"Stacey has her first showing at the art gallery this weekend."

"Art gallery?" Dan asked. "Stacey who?"

"Stacey Gormin ... Mel's sister."

"Aw, Christ. I don't want to go to an art gallery."

"We have to go. It will be fun."

"Whenever you have to tell me something is going to be fun, it never is."

"We can buy a piece for one of these bare walls of yours."

"A piece of what?"

"A painting."

"I gotta buy something?"

"Well, we should."

"How much is that gonna cost?"

"I don't know." Maxine stared at the empty wall behind the couch. "We can get something to go on the wall over the couch, between the two windows." Maxine's eyes went to the small quilt that was hanging over the back of the couch.

Dan saw where she was looking. *Crap!,* he thought, recalling the morning Melvin Jessup, the red-headed hit man, blew a hole through the back of the couch with his shotgun.

"Why's that quilt on the back of the couch like that?"

"Like what?"

"Like that," Maxine replied, pointing at the quilt. "It's pulled down too far, and off to the side."

"No reason," Dan replied.

Maxine moved toward the couch.

"Wait!" Dan shouted.

Maxine spun around. "What's the matter?"

"We better get going, if you want to get to the jewelry store."

Maxine cocked her head, and then her eyes went back to the couch with the palm tree print. She walked over, grabbed the quilt, and slowly pulled it off the back of the couch. Her jaw dropped. "What the hell happened to my couch?"

"Some guy shot it."

"Some guy shot it? What guy?"

Dan pointed a thumb in the direction of the plywood that covered the broken picture window. "The same guy who went through the front window. He was a hitman named Melvin Jessup."

"*Was* a hit man?" Maxine asked. "What do you mean, was a hit man?"

"Rick and some other officers turned him into Swiss cheese."

"Oh."

"Yeah, so he's no longer a problem."

"You told me kids did that."

"That was kind of a fib."

"A fib."

"Yes."

"Why did this man shoot my couch?"

"It was an accident; he was trying to shoot Red and me."

"You told me not much went on here while I was away."

"Also a fib."

Maxine stared at her idiot fiancé. "That's two fibs since I've been home. Is there anything else you need to tell me?"

Dan scratched his chin and his eyes darted skyward in thought. He stared at the hole in the ceiling. "I think that's it," he said.

"Good," Maxine said, "We'll go to the furniture store after the jewelry store and you can help me pick out a new sofa."

"Yes, ma'am."

"No more fibs. Agreed?"

"Agreed."

Maxine turned and started toward the kitchen.

"Wait," Dan said.

Maxine turned back. "What?"

Dan pointed at the ceiling. "There's a hole in the ceiling too."

Maxine looked up. She walked to a spot directly below the damaged sheetrock and peered into the dark hole above. "Did it go all the way through the roof?" she asked.

"Nope."

Maxine shrugged. "Well, I guess that's a good thing."

Dan smiled big. "I love how you can always make lemonade out of shotgun blasts."

Maxine glared at Dan. "And I love how often you give me the opportunity to do so."

"You're welcome."

Chapter Three

"We should bring Mel to the opening," said Maxine, as Dan drove his Porsche down Truman Avenue.

It was a cloudy day and looked like rain, but Dan had the top down as usual. He was fooling around with the radio, switching from Radio Margaritaville to No Shoes Radio. Chris Stapleton was singing "Tennessee Whiskey." Dan sat back in his seat and tapped his thumb on his thigh to the beat of the music.

"Opening of what?" he asked.

"Stacey's art showing."

"Oh, that." Dan took a right onto Duvall Street.

"Did you forget we talked about it this morning?"

"No, but I was hoping if I didn't mention it again, you'd forget about it."

"That's not very nice. We should go and show our support."

"You should just go with some friends."

"I'm going with my *best* friend."

"Thank God! Now I don't have to go."

Maxine shot daggers at Dan. "*You're* my best friend," she said.

"Oh."

"Oh?"

"Oh."

"Don't you have something to say to me?"

Dan thought for a second. "Thanks?"

"Thanks?"

Dan pulled to the curb in front of H&L Diamonds. "This the place?"

"Yes," Maxine answered. "What do you mean, thanks?"

"I don't know. Thanks for saying I'm your best friend."

"Aren't I your best friend?"

Crap! Dan thought. *Proceed with caution.* "You're *one* of my best friends."

"One of them?"

"Well, Red is probably my best friend. I've known him longer than I've known you. We've spent a lot more time together. We have a lot in common, him and me. We're closer in age. We like the same—"

"Stop," Maxine ordered, putting up a hand. She pulled the door lever and climbed out of the Porsche and slammed the door so hard, the whole car shook. She paused just long enough to threaten Dan with an "I'll remember that" before stomping toward the entrance. Dan watched as she yanked the door with such force that it got stuck in the open position. An exiting customer had to abruptly sidestep Maxine as she stormed inside.

"This is gonna cost me," Dan grumbled, as he got out of the car and followed her inside the teal colored clapboard storefront, freeing the stuck door as he did.

Maxine was already eyeing diamonds through the top of one of the glass display cases when Dan walked up and stood beside her. "Whatcha looking at there, friend?" he joked.

Maxine stayed focused on the rocks before her. "Shut up," she said.

"Love you."

"Yeah."

The owner of the place, a man in his mid-fifties with short black hair, parted on the side, was on the other side of the room helping the only other customer in the place. Dan looked over at him. The tall, thin man smiled and nodded his head, as he showed a necklace to the young woman he was assisting. Dan nodded back, and then returned his attention to the case full of engagement rings.

"There's no prices on any of these things," Dan pointed out.

"If you have to ask, you can't afford it," Maxine replied. "But we both know you can afford it." Maxine jabbed Dan playfully in the ribs. "Ain't that right, lottery boy?"

Dan continued to inspect the jewelry, but his thoughts suddenly strayed to prenuptial agreements.

"Don't you think?" Maxine asked.

"What?" Dan asked.

"Weren't you listening to me?"

"Yes."

"What did I say?"

"Something about Stacey's artwork ... or something?"

"That's what I thought." Maxine pointed through the display case. "I like that one," she said.

Maxine was pointing at an 18k gold ring with three princess cut diamonds. The smile on her face and the gleam in her eye told Dan that it was probably the ring she had dreamed of her entire life.

"Do you think it's too big?" Maxine asked.

"No," Dan replied. His voice cracked a little.

"Are you sure? I don't want it to look foolish on my finger."

"I, uh—"

"Good afternoon," said the store's proprietor. "Welcome to H&L Diamonds, I'm Herkle French. Looking at the princess cut, I see. It's a beautiful ring."

"Yes, it is." Maxine agreed.

"Can I take it out for you?" the man asked.

"Ya do, and I'll slap ya," Dan joked. His juvenile humor fell on deaf ears.

The jeweler was already sliding open the glass panel and reaching inside before he even finished his sentence, and Maxine already had her left hand extended, the third finger slightly elevated.

"How much is it?" Dan asked.

Herkle ignored his question. He was not about to reveal the price until Maxine saw it on her finger.

Maxine took the ring and slid it on. She held her hand out in front of her and moved it around to catch the light and see it sparkle, and sparkle it did. "Oh. My. God," she gasped. "Dan, just look at it."

"How much is it?" Dan asked again.

"This ring is twenty-two thousand."

Dan felt his colon rumble and his sphincter tighten. "Dollars?" he asked, his voice rising to a Barry Gibb-ish falsetto.

"Yes," Herkle said with a grin, "dollars."

"Are those metric dollars?" Dan asked.

"Dan," Maxine scolded. She continued to stare at the ring. "I love it."

"She loves it, Dan," said Herkle. He stared at Dan and cocked his head. He had a slight grin that made Dan feel as though he was being taunted. "Dan," he repeated. "I've seen you somewhere before. On the news, perhaps. A little mishap on Christmas morning, wasn't it? Crashed your Porsche into a block wall, if I remember correctly."

"Yeah, that's me," said Dan.

"Yeah, that's him," Maxine repeated disgustedly.

"I'm also the guy who rescued that little Cuban girl from her kidnappers," said Dan.

"Really? Sorry, I don't remember that."

"Of course not."

The entrance door opened and the owner stepped back. Dan looked up at the jeweler's fearful, widening eyes. "What's the matter with—" Dan turned around, and

29

standing in the middle of the room was a man in a ski mask.

The masked man was holding a chrome .38 revolver in one hand and a small canvas bag in the other. He was dressed in a pair of blue jeans and a black Members Only jacket zipped up as far as it would go.

"This is a stick up!" the guy shouted. He jockeyed his head around, trying to make the collar of his jacket more comfortable for his fat neck and second chin. "Move away from that silent alarm!"

Herkle glanced down at the floor to his right at a red round button that was positioned just under the display case.

"I said move away from it!"

The jeweler slowly sidestepped to his left, cowardly putting Maxine between him and the gunman. Maxine was frozen.

Dan showed his hands. "We'll do whatever you ask, pal," he said.

"I know you will," said the robber. He tossed the bag over Maxine's head to Herkle. "Fill that up." He trained the gun on Maxine. "I'll start with that rock you got on your finger."

Maxine looked down at the ring. "But, it's mine."

"Give him the ring, Maxine," Dan said.

"But—"

"Give him the damn ring."

Maxine slid the ring off her finger.

"Toss it to me," said the man.

Maxine did as she was told. The robber shoved the ring into his front pocket. "Hurry up!" he shouted at the jeweler.

Herkle was moving as fast as he could to fill the bag. When it was almost full, he tossed it back to the guy.

The gunman grinned big through the mouth hole of his mask, and saluted. "It was nice doing business with you." He shoved his weapon into the front of his waistband, turned, and ran out the door.

"My ring," Maxine sobbed.

The jeweler leapt onto the silent alarm button.

Dan looked at Maxine's face. *Dammit*! he thought, and ran for the door.

"No!" Maxine shouted, but it was too late.

When Dan got to the sidewalk he noticed the ski mask lying on the concrete. He looked up Duvall Street to his right and then to his left. He caught sight of the black jacket rounding the corner onto Greene Street. Dan took off running. He could already hear the sirens off in the distance.

The thief turned down an alley behind Sloppy Joe's and then cut through the parking lot behind the Key West Chamber of Commerce. Dan was closing the gap between them; his recent morning runs had paid off.

When the thug reached Caroline Street, Dan was only twenty-five yards behind him. That's as far as the guy made it. As he turned and pulled his weapon from his waistband, he was struck by a navy blue Mercedes. He rolled onto the hood and up and over the roof, landing on the blacktop. The Mercedes slowed and pulled to the curb.

The would be robber tried to get up and run, but the jagged piece of fibula sticking through the hole in his pant leg assured he wouldn't.

Dan reached the guy and shoved him back to the ground. The guy screamed out in pain. Dan walked across Caroline Street and picked up the .38 that had come to rest against the curb. He turned and walked back over to the guy.

"Where's the bag of jewelry?" Dan asked.

"My leg!" the guy shouted. "My leg." He thrashed around on the pavement like a beached marlin.

Dan put his foot on the guy's leg and pushed down. He gave vent to an anguished cry that sounded uncannily like the one Charlie Brown made when he missed the football kick and landed flat on his back. Dan had to smile at that.

"Where's the bag?" Dan demanded.

"Screw you!" the thug hissed through gritted teeth.

Dan reached into his front pocket and pulled out Maxine's ring. Then he noticed the bulge in the guy's jacket. Dan unzipped the jacket and reached inside; there, he found the canvas bag. Dan rose up and saluted the guy. "Nice doing business with you," he said. Dan turned and walked back the way he had come.

When Dan arrived back at the jewelry store there were four cop cars parked out front with their light bars flashing. Several uniformed officers were in the street and on the sidewalk. Dan was stopped at the door by one of the cops.

"You can't go in, Coast," said the officer. "The place was just robbed."

Dan held up the bag. "Yeah, I know. I was here when it happened." Dan pushed past the officer and went inside. He held the bag in the air. "Got your shit back," he announced. He tossed the bag onto the display case and laid the gun down beside it. Then he reached into his pocket for Maxine's ring. "Wrap this up, we'll take it."

Maxine threw her arms around Dan and squeezed him tightly. "Why did you run after him?" she asked. "You could have been killed."

"I had to get the ring," Dan replied. "Not every woman has a story like this to tell about the day she got her engagement ring."

Maxine took the ring and put it back on her finger. "You're right," she agreed. "This will make a great story to tell our children someday."

Dan felt his sphincter tighten once again. "Children?" he asked.

Maxine smiled up at him. "Or grandchildren."

"Grandchildren?" Dan sidestepped to the display case to steady himself. "I'm not feeling so good."

"It's probably all the excitement," said Maxine.

"Yeah, that's probably it."

"Will that be cash or credit?" the jeweler asked.

Dan reached into his pocket for his credit card. He tossed it onto the glass top. "How much did you say it was, French?"

"Twenty-two," said Herkle.

"How much is it after I risked my life to chase down the guy who had just robbed you and got all your shit back?"

33

"Still twenty-two."

"Seriously? You're giving me nothing off?"

"You didn't have to run after the robber," he sniffed. "I have insurance."

"Maybe we'll just go somewhere else then," Dan stated.

"No we won't," Maxine chimed in. "Ring it up, French. I'll wear it home."

Chapter Four

Later that afternoon Dan relaxed in one of the Adirondack chairs next to the fire pit. A lit Dominican cigar hung out the corner of his mouth. He had a tequila, Seven, and lime in his hand, and the morning edition of the Key West Citizen folded and lying in his lap. Maxine sat in the other chair, directly across from him. His semi-faithful canine lay at his side in the dirt.

Dan took a long drag on his cigar and blew smoke rings into the air, then he took a sip of his drink. He glanced over at Maxine. She had a glass of wine in her right hand and was still staring at the ring on her left. The smile hadn't left her face since the purchase. Dan liked seeing her this happy, but holy shit, that was a lot of money for a rock glued to a thin piece of metal. He sipped his drink again.

"What are you smiling about?" Dan asked, already knowing the answer.

"I love my ring," Maxine responded.

"I would hope so."

"Was it too much?"

"Yes, but you're worth it."

Maxine jumped out of the chair and hugged Dan for the tenth time since receiving the ring. "Thank you." She kissed him on the cheek. "I love you."

"Back at ya."

Maxine rose up and turned toward the house.

"Where are you going?" Dan asked.

"I have to call my mom and tell her. I haven't told anyone in my family yet." Maxine held her hand out in front of her and admired the ring as she skipped up the gravel path to the house.

Dan watched her until the screen door closed behind her. He puffed on his cigar a few more times and took another drink of his tequila. He put the glass on the ground next to his chair and went back to reading the morning's funnies.

"Son of a bitch!" Dan heard someone shout from behind him. He turned his head to see his new neighbor wiping her shoe vigorously on the grass; she glared at Dan as she did so.

"Learning a new dance step?" Dan called out.

"Very funny," the woman returned. "There's dog shit all over this backyard. Probably from that mutt of yours."

Buddy lifted his head and looked at the woman. Dan reached down and patted the dog's head. "Don't worry about it, pal. She sounds a little nutty."

"Isn't there a leash law in this town?" asked the woman.

"I'm sure there is," Dan replied.

Buddy dropped his head and shut his eyes.

"Well, then, why isn't that mongrel on one?" she asked.

"I was wondering the same thing about you," Dan answered.

"You're a real asshole."

"I never said I wasn't."

"You have a comeback for everything, don't you?"

"I'm gonna say yes to that."

The woman shook her head. "Just get this yard cleaned up. I shouldn't have to put up with shit like this."

"What kind of shit would you prefer?"

Dan saw the woman's fists clench at her sides. When she spoke she sounded like she was biting the heads off ten penny nails. "Clean. It. *Up*."

"Clean it up … or?"

"Or, I'll call the police."

"Now I'm really scared."

The woman turned and headed for the back door. When she was almost there, she turned back. "And that cigar stinks as bad as the dog shit. I can smell it all the way in the house."

"Well, lucky you," Dan responded. "I had to pay eight bucks to smell this thing, and you get to do it for free."

The woman gave an exasperated squeal. She said, as she stomped up the steps and stood for a moment in the back door. "You're impossible!!" she screamed, and slammed the door. Dan heard the windows rattle and winced.

Dan went back to his paper. "Sounds like someone's having a bad vacation," he mumbled.

Maxine stuck her head out the kitchen door. "Were you calling me?"

"No," Dan replied.

"I thought I heard you say something."

"I was talking to the nice lady next door."

"Oh, you met her?"

"You could say that."

"She was nice?"

"No, she was a bitch."

Maxine walked out onto the steps. "What was she bitching about?"

"She thinks Buddy shit in her backyard."

"Did he?"

"Probably."

"Are you going to clean it up?"

"Nope."

"Shouldn't you?"

"Yup." Dan's attention went out past the house to the street. Julian Thompson was riding his bike. "Hey!" Dan shouted.

Julian's head snapped around. He stopped his bike and jumped off the seat. "Did you call me?" Julian shouted.

"Yeah," Dan yelled back. "Come here for a second."

The ten-year-old jumped back on his bike, turned, and pedaled down Dan's driveway and into the backyard. "What's up, Dan?" he asked. "Hey, Buddy," he said to the dog.

"You want to make a couple bucks?" Dan asked.

"What do I gotta do?"

"Get the shovel out of the shed and scoop up the dog shit in the neighbor's yard."

"Your yard too?"

Dan glanced around the yard. "Yeah, do mine too … and Bev's."

"How much?"

"Five bucks?"

"Ten," Julian countered.

"Eight."

"Ten."

Maxine looked on as the negotiation continued.

"Fine, ten," Dan said defeatedly.

Julian went to the shed and grabbed a pointed shovel. "That's ten a week," he said.

"Ten a week?"

"Yeah. For ten bucks, I'll do it twice a week."

"Fine."

"Good job, Julian," said Maxine. "Take him for all you can." She turned around and stepped back into the kitchen.

"Where do you want me to put the poop?" Julian asked.

"See if that BMW's door is unlocked and throw it on the front seat," Dan replied.

"Seriously?"

"No, not seriously."

"Her car's not there anyway."

Dan stretched his neck to see the driveway. "She must have left. There's a roll of plastic garbage bags in the shed on a shelf. Put the *poop* in one of them and tie it shut. Just leave it by the shed."

Julian went back to the shed for a bag and then strolled into the neighbor's yard and began scooping. "Who moved in?" Julian asked.

"Some bitch," Dan replied.

Julian snickered. "Did she buy the place, or is she just renting?"

"I hope she's just renting."

"Do you think she's—"

"Less chatter, more work, kid," Dan said, and returned to his newspaper.

A few minutes later Julian walked over to Bev's yard in search of more dog logs. When he finished there, he did Dan's yard, tied the bag closed, and dropped it next to the shed. "Anything else?" he asked.

"Nope," Dan replied.

Julian held out his hand.

"What?" Dan asked.

"Can I have my money?" asked Julian.

"Payday's on Friday," Dan said. "And I hold back a week."

Julian stared at Dan.

"What?" Dan asked.

"You're a dick," Julian responded.

"Hey! Is that any way for a ten-year-old to talk?"

"It is when they're talking to you."

Dan laughed and reached into his pocket for his money clip. "I'm just bustin' your tiny little balls, kid." Dan peeled a twenty-dollar bill off the top of the stack and handed it to the young boy. "There's this week and next. What day ya comin' back?"

"How about Mondays and Thursdays?"

"Sounds good."

Julian ran for his bike. "Thanks, Dan!"

Shit, Dan thought as he watched the boy pedal away. *I should have made him get me another drink before he left.*

"How did he do?" Maxine asked through the screen.

"Good," Dan replied. "Hey, were you planning on getting me an engagement present?"

Maxine cocked her head. "Like what?"

Dan rattled the ice in his glass. "I could use another drink."

Chapter Five

"Hey, are you awake?" Maxine asked.

"What?" Dan asked, his voice grumbled with early morning phlegm.

"Are you awake?"

He cleared his throat. "I am now," he replied.

"Did you hear that noise?"

"You mean besides you asking if I was awake?" Dan turned his head to see the clock; it was 3:07.

"It was a clunk."

"A clunk? What's a clunk?"

"The sound. It was kind of like a clunk."

"What makes a clunk sound at three in the morning?" Dan asked.

"I don't know. That's what I want you to go see."

Dan rolled over and pulled the blanket up over his shoulder. "If it was anything, the dog would be barking."

"Can you go see, please?"

"Ugh!" Dan whipped back the covers and jumped out of bed and headed for the hall.

"Aren't you going to put some pants on?"

"No."

Dan walked naked down the hall and into the dining room. He peered through the doorway into the kitchen; the back door was closed. He looked around the living room. Buddy was sound asleep on his flannel bed next to the small wooden table that displayed a small framed photograph of Alex, Dan's deceased wife.

"Hey," Dan said. "Hey, dog!"

Buddy raised his head and looked at his best friend.

"You hear a clunk?" Dan asked.

Buddy didn't answer.

A light came on outside, and Dan's attention went to the window behind the couch. He craned his neck to get a better look as he made his way through the darkness toward the window. The car next door was backing out of the driveway. Dan tried to get a look at the driver, but it was too dark. He watched as the car backed into the street and drove away. Dan's eyes went from window to window of the house next door. One window, which Dan knew to be the living room, was dimly lit.

Dan shrugged his shoulders at the absence of evidence of any obvious thing that may have made a clunking sound. He went to the front door and stared out the glass panel. *All good*, he thought. He went to the back door and did the same thing.

When Dan climbed back into bed, Maxine was already asleep. "Hey," he whispered. "Hey!" a little louder.

"What?" Maxine asked.

"You awake?"

"I am now. Did you see anything?"

"I didn't see any clunks, if that's what you mean."

"Good," said Maxine. "That's all we need, a bunch of clunks running around the yard this early in the morning."

Dan lay on his back with his fingers laced behind his head. He watched the blades on the ceiling fan as they slowly spun above him. "I can't sleep."

"Close your eyes."

"You know what would make me sleep?"

"What would that be?"

"Another engagement present."

"I thought the drink I made you was your gift."

"Did you really think it would end there?"

"No. What do you want? You want me to make you another drink?"

"I was thinking more along the lines of a sex gift."

"You were, were you?"

"Yup."

Maxine reached over and took hold of his manhood. "It doesn't seem like you're ready for—oh there it is."

Chapter Six

A few minutes after seven the smell of bacon opened Dan's eyes. He breathed in deeply. It was good to have Maxine home.

He pulled back the covers and threw his legs over the edge of the bed. Grabbing a pair of running shorts out of the bottom drawer, he slid them on, then searched for a T-shirt. He settled on an old concert T he had had for over thirty years: The Fixx—Reach the Beach.

Dan left the bedroom and walked into the kitchen. He walked up behind Maxine, put his arms around her, and pressed his nose into the nape of her neck. "You smell great," he said.

"That's the bacon," she replied.

"I wonder why they don't make a bacon-scented perfume."

"No man would be able to function in the work place if all the women smelled like bacon."

"I bet it would even be some form of sexual harassment to tell them they smell delicious." Dan kissed Maxine's neck. He turned toward the coffee maker. "Too bad there's no men's cologne that smells like a brand new Coach handbag. You women wouldn't be able to keep your stinking paws off us."

Maxine sniffed the air. "Speaking of stinking ... you're a little ripe. Maybe you should jump in the shower before breakfast."

"Is it turning you on?" Dan said hopefully.

"Not at all."

Dan took a deep whiff of one arm pit, shrugged, and reached into the cabinet for a coffee mug and poured himself a cup.

With a pair of tongs, Maxine removed each piece of bacon from the frying pan, one at a time, and laid them neatly on a paper towel she had placed on the counter top. "How do you want your eggs?" she asked.

"Over-medium," Dan replied. "But why don't we leave the bacon right where it is, go for a run together, and then eat after we get back?"

"Are you serious?"

"Yeah. Why?"

"We don't run together."

"Maybe it's time we started."

Maxine lay the tongs down next to the bacon. "Okay. Let me change into some running clothes." She kissed Dan on the lips and trotted off to the bedroom to change. "Be right back."

Dan walked to the front door and picked up his sneakers, along with the socks he had worn the last time he ran. He settled in his recliner and put them on. He reached for the remote control and turned on the television. A classic episode of *The Brady Bunch* was playing on MeTV. He sat back in the chair and watched. "Pork chops and applesauce," Dan whispered to himself in his best Peter Brady doing his best Bogart impression.

What the hell is she doing? Dan thought. It had been twenty minutes since she said, "Be right back." He stood and went down the hall. Maxine was putting on eye makeup in the bathroom mirror.

"What's taking so long?" Dan asked.

"I'm getting ready," Maxine replied.

"You're going for a run, not entering a beauty contest."

"Funny. I still want to look nice."

"You looked fine before."

"Fine?"

"You know what I mean."

"I wanted to look better than fine."

"What the Christ?" Dan mumbled.

"What was that?"

"Nothing." Dan turned and was halfway down the hall when Maxine announced that she was all set. "Thank God."

"What?" Maxine called out."

"Nothing."

The two runners walked down the front steps together and stood on the sidewalk. Maxine stretched as Dan stared at the house next door. The car Dan had seen leave in the early morning hours was still gone.

"What are you staring at?" Maxine asked.

"Nothing," Dan replied.

"You ready?"

"Yut."

Maxine started running and Dan followed. As they ran past the front door of the neighbor's house, Dan noticed it was ajar; he stopped running. Maxine looked back and saw Dan walking up the sidewalk that led to the front door; she halted as well, and turned around.

"What are you doing?" asked Maxine.

Dan put up his index finger. "Hold on," he said. When he got to the door, he peered through the three inch gap into the darkness.

"What are you doing?" Maxine asked again. She was suddenly behind him.

Dan flinched. "Christ. Don't sneak up behind me like that." He gently pushed open the door with his fingertips. It made a creaking sound until it came to rest with the doorknob against the wall behind it. "Hello?" he called out.

Dan walked cautiously up the three steps and stood in the doorway. "Hello? Anyone here?" He turned back to Maxine. "Wait out here." He stepped inside.

The modest two-story bungalow had an open floor plan that converged on the living room. Beyond the living room was a small dining area. At the back of the house was the kitchen. The down stairs was set up similar to Dan's house, with the exception being, there was no wall separating the dining area and kitchen, and there were two bedrooms and a second bath upstairs. To Dan's right, against the far wall was a staircase. Dan knew the layout of the house, having been in the home on one other occasion, two years earlier, when he helped the homeowner, Lou Stewart, install a new dishwasher in the kitchen and an electrical outlet in one of the bedrooms upstairs.

The room was dark. All the shades and blinds were closed, except one. In front of the window with the open shade was a round three-legged table, and upon it was placed a small Tiffany lamp. Strange—at 3:00 a.m. the lamp was lit, now it was turned off. Dan walked to the center of the dining area, looked around, and then went to the staircase.

"Hey, is anybody here?" Dan called up the stairs.

"I don't think anyone is here," said Maxine.

"Jesus Christ!" Dan shouted, grabbing his chest. "I just asked you not to sneak up on me like that."

Maxine giggled. "Sorry."

"And I told you to wait outside."

"You're not the boss of me, Jumpy Jumperton."

Just then the two heard a car door slam. Both their heads turned toward the open front door.

"What was that?" Dan asked.

"Sounded like a car door, Jumpy."

"Quit with the Jumpy," Dan warned. He made his way back to the door to see Chief of Police Rick Carver standing at the bottom of Edna McGee's front steps. Edna stood on her porch speaking with Rick.

"It's Carver," said Dan. He instinctively closed the door a hair or two, while leaving a gap to spy through.

"What's he doing?" Maxine asked.

"He's talking to old lady McGee." Dan moved closer to the door. He could see Rick's white Bronco parked in front of McGee's house.

"What are we gonna do?" Maxine asked.

"We'll just wait in here till he leaves."

"What if Stewart's tenant comes back."

"We'll cross the bridge when it's time."

"Wow."

"What?"

"You're starting to sound like Red. It's 'We'll cross that bridge when we come to it.'"

"You know what I meant," Dan snapped back. He continued to watch Chief Carver through the open door. Suddenly Edna McGee pointed at the Stewart house. "Shit."

"What's the matter?" Maxine tried to look over Dan's shoulder. "What's going on?"

"McGee just pointed over here," said Dan.

"Do you think she saw us come in here?"

"Probably. The nosy old bat sees everything."

Rick gave a slight wave, turned, and headed toward the Stewart's house.

"Dammit," said Dan. "Here he comes."

"What do we do?"

"Out the back door!"

Dan and Maxine turned and headed as quickly as they could through the dining room, into the kitchen, and out the back door. Dan pulled the door shut quietly behind him.

"Where do we go?" Maxine asked.

"My house," answered Dan.

The two headed across the yard.

"Hey!" Rick called out.

Dan and Maxine stopped dead in their tracks. Rick was standing in the driveway.

"Hey, Rick," said Dan.

"What are you two doing?" Rick asked.

"Checking for dog shit," Maxine replied.

Dan shot her a look of approval and then returned his attention to Rick. "The tenant complained that Buddy was shitting in her yard, so we came over to look."

Rick looked at their empty hands. "Where's your bag, and what were you going to scoop it with?"

"We were just looking to see if there was really any dog crap over there," said Dan.

"Is that a two-man job?" Rick asked.

"Well, we were going to go for a run afterward," Maxine explained.

Rick folded his beefy, sunburned forearms across his chest. "After you inspected the dog shit." Rick said.

"Yes," Dan responded.

"Was there any?" Rick asked.

"Any what?" Dan asked.

"Dog crap."

"None at all," Maxine replied.

"The lady's a nut job," said Dan.

"Who's the tenant?" Rick asked.

"Some lady," Dan said.

"She got a name?" Rick asked.

"Probably," Dan replied. "I can't imagine anyone going through life without a name." He walked toward Rick and Maxine followed.

Rick ignored Dan's stupid attempt at humor; he was used to it. "The front door is open."

Dan feigned ignorance. "Oh yeah? Weird."

"And your neighbor across the street said she saw you and Maxine go inside the house."

"Ah, she's crazy too," Dan said, making a circular motion around his ear with his index finger. "She probably just saw us walking down the driveway."

"She drinks too," Maxine added, pretending her thumb was a bottle of booze.

Rick turned and walked back around to the front of the house. He walked up the steps and into the house. Dan followed him to the top of the steps.

"Hello?" Rick called out. "Key West Police Department."

"There's no one here," said Dan.

"How do you know?"

"Saw the car leave earlier."

"What time was that?"

"Around three this morning."

Rick reached to his right and flipped on a wall switch. The light on the ceiling fan came on and illuminated the room. "Hello?" he hollered one more time. "When did she complain about the dog crap?"

"Yesterday afternoon," Dan said.

"That all you talked about?"

"No. She also told me my cigar was stinking up the place."

"What kind of cigar?"

"Dominican ... a Montecristo."

"Those usually smell pretty good."

"Yeah, she was just being a bitch."

"That's all you argued about?"

"We didn't argue. I just told her she was lucky to smell it for free, because I had to pay eight bucks for it."

Rick grinned. "That's pretty funny." He reached up and removed his gold-rimmed aviators and slid them into his shirt pocket.

"I thought so too," Dan agreed.

Rick walked to the stairs and started up to the second floor.

"Where ya going?" Dan asked.

"Have a look around."

"Are you supposed to do that?"

"I'm the Chief of Police, I can do anything I want."

Dan waited as Rick went upstairs. He turned back to see Maxine through the open door, sitting on the front steps; she was staring at her cell phone. He wondered if it was Facebook or Instagram. Maxine held her phone out away from her and snapped a selfie. *Snapchat*, he surmised. *Would she be a rabbit, a cat, or a unicorn this time?*, he wondered.

"Dan!" Rick hollered.

"Yeah?" Dan shouted back.

"Can you come up here for a second?"

"Sure." Dan walked up the stairs. At the top was a bathroom; Dan glanced inside. He turned and saw Rick standing at the doorway of one of the bedrooms. He was staring at the floor.

"What's up?" Dan asked.

"You ever see this guy before?"

Dan walked down the hallway toward him. He looked over Rick's shoulder into the bedroom. Lying on the hardwood floor was the lifeless body of a fifty-something male. He was dressed in nothing but a bathrobe.

"Nope," Dan replied. "I've never seen that man in my life."

"Are you sure?"

"Pretty sure."

"Pretty sure?"

"Well, I mean … he doesn't look familiar."

"What time did you say the car left this morning?"

"Around three."

"What were you doing up at three?"

"Maxine thought she heard something, so I got up to check. A car's headlights caught my eye, and when I looked out my living room window, I saw her back out and drive down the street."

"You saw her?"

"Well, I assumed it was her."

Rick looked back down at the dead guy. "It sure wasn't him."

"We don't know that for sure."

"What do you mean?"

"That was almost five hours ago I heard the car leave. He could have come back at some point."

"Did you hear a car come back?"

"No."

"But you didn't see who was driving when the car left at three."

"No, but I assumed it was the woman who was staying here."

"She's the only one you saw here?"

"Yut."

"Never saw her with a man?"

"Nope."

Rick got down on one knee and laid two fingers against the side of the man's neck. He could tell he was already dead, but it didn't hurt to make sure. "What did Maxine say she heard?"

"A clunk."

"A clunk?" Rick carefully opened the man's robe to inspect as much of his body as he could without contaminating the crime scene. "No entry wounds that I can see," he said. Rick stood and reached for his two-way radio. He keyed the mic. "Angie, it's Chief Carver."

"Go ahead, Chief," came Angie's voice over the speaker.

"Can you send a couple units over to 634 Beach View Street? Also notify the crime scene unit and the coroner's office. We got a body over here."

"10-4, Chief. Out."

"You were saying, a clunk," said Rick.

"Yeah," Dan answered. "I figured she heard the car door slam."

"You didn't hear anything?"

"No."

"What kind of car?"

"BMW ... green."

Rick turned and walked past Dan and back down the hall. "Come on," he said. "Let's get downstairs."

When the two men got back downstairs to the dining room, Dan glanced over at the small Tiffany lamp. "Hey," he said. "If that man upstairs was dead before the car left, then someone else was in the house *after* the car left."

"What makes you say that?" Rick asked.

Dan pointed at the lamp. "Because that lamp was lit at three, but then it was off when we came inside ... you and me, I mean."

Rick shot Dan an *I know you're lying* glance, and then walked over to the small table that held the lamp. He bent over and looked underneath the table. "Great theory, Sherlock, but the lamp is on a timer."

"Oh," Dan responded. "I didn't notice that."

"That's why you're supposed to leave the investigating to the professionals."

"Yeah, yeah," said Dan, and the duo stepped outside.

"What were you guys doing in there?" Maxine asked.

"Checking out the awesome dead body lying on the bedroom floor upstairs," Dan said.

Maxine chuckled. "Good one." She glanced over at Rick; he wasn't smiling. "He's joking, right?"

Rick shook his head no. "I'm afraid not."

"Is it the woman who bitched about the dog shit and your cigar?" Maxine asked.

"No," Dan replied.

"The victim is a male," said Rick.

The first patrol car pulled up in front a few seconds later, followed by another, and then another. Rick walked down the steps to speak with the officers. He stood with his back to Dan and Maxine; they couldn't hear what he was saying. Rick pointed down the street, and then up the street. He pointed in Dan's backyard, and then over at Edna McGee's house. Rick was an expert pointer.

One of the officers walked down the driveway and into the backyard; another headed for Edna McGee's. A third officer turned and walked over to two other officers who were standing nearby; that officer began pointing as though he was a graduate of the Rick Carver School of Pointing. Rick turned and walked back to Dan and Maxine.

"Coroner should be here any second," Rick remarked.

"What do you want us to do?" Dan asked.

Rick stared at his friend as he removed his sunglasses from his shirt pocket and put them on. "What I want you to do, is nothing."

"What do you mean?" Dan asked.

Maxine smirked.

"I don't want you to do anything," Rick repeated. "I don't want you snooping around. I don't want you asking any questions. Do you understand?"

Dan nodded his head.

"When you shake your head, Coast, all I can hear is the rocks rattling," said Rick. "I need to hear you say it. Do. You. Understand?"

"Yes," Dan responded. "I understand."

"Good."

Dan leaned over and looked around Rick. The officer who had walked over to Edna's was now on his way back across the street.

"Hey, Chief," said the cop.

Rick turned. "Yeah, what is it, Bobby?" he asked.

"Chief, the old woman across the street says she never saw a car over here or heard anything at all unusual this morning."

"You're shittin' me," said Dan. "She sees everything."

The cop shrugged. "She said she had no idea that anyone had rented the place. She said the only ones she saw over here were those two." The cop nodded his head in Dan and Maxine's direction.

"Same goes for the old man across the street there," said another officer, as he pointed back at Mr. Stein's house. "Said he hasn't seen anyone over here since the Stewarts left three months ago."

Rick turned back to Dan and Maxine. "Please tell me you saw someone, Maxine."

Maxine looked at Dan, then back at Rick.

"Tell him, Maxine," said Dan.

"I never saw anyone," Maxine replied.

"What do you mean?" asked Dan. "What about when she was moving in and you asked me why I was looking out the window?"

"I never looked out," said Maxine. "I just took your word that someone was moving in."

"What about when she yelled at me about the dog shit, and the cigar?"

"Never saw her then either."

Dan threw up his arms. "That's just great. You're telling me that I'm the only one who saw someone moving in here that day?"

"Sorry," said Maxine.

Dan looked down and stared at the step below him. "This doesn't make any sense, someone must have seen her. How about the Stewarts? Get a hold of them. They must know who they rented the place to."

Rick put up his hand. "Calm down, Coast. I'll make that call as soon as I get back to the station. I can get their number from the real estate company that handles the rentals. I'm sure we'll get this all figured out."

"Well I should hope so," Dan responded.

Maxine stood up from the steps. "Is it okay to go for our run now, Rick?" she asked.

"I don't feel like going for a run now," said Dan.

"It'll clear your head," Maxine argued.

"My head is perfectly clear, Maxine."

"He's right, Maxine," said Rick. "His head has been completely clear of anything since I met him."

Maxine chuckled; so did a few cops within ear shot.

Dan stood and started for his own home. "Yeah, laugh it up, everyone."

Maxine followed him, and just as they got to their front steps, an unmarked car pulled up. Two plain-clothes detectives exited the car and walked over to Rick. Dan watched from his front porch as Rick filled the detectives in on the situation.

"I need a drink," Dan grumbled. He turned to open his door, and stepping over the door mat that read THE COASTS, he went inside.

Chapter Seven

"Four days," Red Baxter announced, as Dan walked through the front doors of Red's Bar and Grill. Red stood behind the bar. He had a bar rag draped over his left shoulder. In his left hand he gripped a bar glass.

Dan crossed the floor, his flip-flops sticking to the dried beer and soda, as usual. Jimmy Buffett's "Come Monday" played on the old Wurlitzer.

"Four days, what?" Dan asked, as he climbed aboard his favorite orange barstool.

Red was bent over searching for something under the bar. "Four days since you've been here," came his muffled reply.

"I didn't know you kept track." Dan heard the jangling of jostled glasses as Red continued his noisy search. "What the hell are you looking for?"

Red straightened up; his round face was flushed and sweaty. "My goddamn bar rag. I just had it in my hand, and now it's dropped off the face of the earth."

"Are you talking about the bar rag that's hanging over your shoulder?"

Red turned his head and looked down at the white cotton rag. "Goddammit!" He yanked the rag off his shoulder and began polishing the glass.

"They say the memory is the first thing to go," said Dan.

"Yeah, well, they're wrong about that," Red argued. "What can I get ya?"

"The usge."

"Usge?"

"It's short for 'the usual'. All the kids are saying it."

"I'd rather *you* didn't. You sound like an idiot."

"I guess you're right, we wouldn't want both of us sounding like idiots."

"You got that righ—hey!"

"Tequila, Seven, and lime."

Red scooped up some ice in the glass he was polishing, added a shot of tequila, and filled it the rest of the way with 7UP. After returning the soda gun to its resting place, he slid the glass across the bar to his friend. "So, how did the ring shopping go?"

"I would say it was painless," Dan replied, "but I think I heard my money clip sobbing last night."

"How much?"

"I'd rather not say."

"I'd rather you did."

"It was more than a buck, but less than a million."

"That narrows it down. What else has been going on?"

"Not much. We found a dead body in the house next door."

Red's jaw dropped. "Dead body? Holy shit. Next door? Bev's?"

"No. The other side."

"Stewart's place?"

"Yeah."

"You found the body?"

"Kinda. Rick actually found it."

"Man or woman?"

"Man."

"It wasn't Mr. Stewart, was it?"

"No, it was someone I've never seen before."

"Was the guy renting from the Stewarts?"

"Don't know."

"What do ya know?"

"Long story short, I saw a woman moving a couple suitcases into the place late Tuesday morning. Tuesday afternoon she came out back and bitched at me about dog shit in her yard and the smell of my cigar smoke. Three o'clock this morning, her car, a green Beamer, backed out of the driveway and took off down the road. This morning around eight, Maxine and I were gonna go for a run. I noticed the Stewart's front door was open. Maxine and I went inside to have a look around. That's when Rick pulled up out front—"

"Long story *short*?" Red asked.

"You want me to finish?"

"Sure."

"We hightailed it out the back door. Rick saw us in the backyard and called us over. He noticed the door was open as well, so Rick and I went in for another look around. He went upstairs and found the guy lying dead on the bedroom floor."

"Was he naked?"

Dan cocked his head. "Odd question. He was in a robe."

"Just a robe?"

"Yes, just a robe."

"Shot? Strangled? Stabbed?"

"No sign of any of that."

"And no sign of the woman?"

"Nope."

"What happened to the suitcases?" Red asked.

"Huh," Dan replied. "Never thought of that."

"She must have put them back in the car," Red surmised.

"Yeah, she must have."

"Hmm." Drifting into deep thought, Red tapped his chin with his index finger "This is definitely a mystery," he said at length. "When do we start the investigation?"

"Rick said I wasn't to do anything. He pretty much told me to keep my nose out of it."

"Oh, okay. So, when do we start the investigation?"

"I'm guessing we already started."

"I think I'd better have a drink too," Red said, and made himself a Scotch and ginger ale.

Chapter Eight

"It's about time," Dan remarked, as Red walked through the front door.

"It's four o'clock," Red replied.

"I said to be here at three-thirty."

"You ain't the boss of me." Red walked across the living room to the dining room and stood next to Dan in front of Dan's large dry-erase board.

At the top of the board Dan had written DEAD GUY/MYSTERY WOMAN. Below that was a timeline starting with Tuesday morning, when Dan first saw the woman taking suitcases out of the car and into the house. There were hash marks along the timeline that were labeled BITCHED ABOUT DOG SHIT, HEARD CLUNKING NOISE, SAW FRONT DOOR OPEN, AND FOUND DEAD GUY. Below the timeline Dan had written GREEN BMW, FLORIDA TAGS, AND MISSING SUITCASES.

"What do we got?" Red asked.

"You're lookin' at it," Dan replied.

"Have you spoken with the Stewarts yet?"

"Rick said he was going to give them a call earlier this morning."

"Shouldn't we give them a call in case Rick doesn't share his information?"

"You're probably right."

"I usually am."

Dan glanced over at his friend. "Really?"

"Well, sometimes."

"That's better." Dan walked to the kitchen. "I got the Stewart's phone number in here somewhere."

Red went straight for Dan's bar, which sat against the wall that separated the kitchen from the dining room. He grabbed himself a glass. "You want a drink?"

"Yut."

Red grabbed a second glass and joined Dan in the kitchen. He opened the freezer. "The ice trays are empty," he said.

Dan was searching through a junk drawer next to the stove. "I guess we'll have warm drinks then."

Red slammed the freezer door. "I hate room temperature drinks," he complained.

"Better than no drinks at all."

Red shrugged. "I guess."

"I know I've got Alice Stewart's cell phone number in here somewhere." Dan shut the junk drawer and opened a second drawer filled with old bills and other paperwork.

"Is this it?" Red asked, pointing at a white piece of paper stuck to the refrigerator door with a Paradise Pizza magnet. "Definitely your shitty handwriting. It says 'Stewart's' with a phone number underneath."

Dan turned around. "No, that's the number of another Stewart I know."

"Huh, what are the odds you—"

"Give me the goddamn number!" Dan snapped.

Red removed the paper from the door and handed it to Dan. "Do you think these Stewarts know the other Stewart's phone number?"

"Shut up, ya moron, and make the drinks."

Dan pulled out his cell and dialed the number.

"Hello?" said a woman on the other end.

"Alice?" Dan asked.

"Yes."

"This is Dan Coast … your neighbor in Key West."

"Yes, Dan. Oh my goodness! Are you and Maxine okay?"

"We're fine, Alice. So I'm guessing you spoke with Chief Carver this morning."

"Yes, he called Lou —— *[crackle]* morning and explained everything."

"Sounds like we have a bad connection, Alice."

"Yes, the reception is *[crackle]* —— spotty up here. You see, Lou and I arc on a cruise in Alaska."

Dan pressed his phone against his chest and remarked to Red: "She's in Alaska. I never talked to anyone in Alaska before. Pretty cool." Red nodded his agreement.

"Did you give him the name of your tenants?" Dan asked Alice.

"That's just it, Dan, those people *[crackle]* —— not our tenants. We hadn't rented *[crackle]* —— place out to anyone because we had planned on coming back next week. We don't know what they were doing there."

"Strange."

"Very *[crackle]* ——"

"What?"

"Very strange."

"Are you coming back early now … because of what has happened?"

"No, we're just going to stick to our original *[crackle]* —— and return next Friday. I told Lou I wanted to head back to Key West, but he said there was nothing we could do about it. I guess he's right."

"Yeah, I guess. Did Rick—Chief Carver ask you if you knew anyone who drove a green BMW?"

"He asked, but we didn't know of anyone. He also emailed Lou photographs of the deceased man to see if *[crackle]* —— one of us recognized him."

"I'm guessing you didn't."

"Right."

"Okay thanks, Alice."

"You're *[crackle]* —— welcome, Dan."

"If I have any more questions, would it be okay to call you back?"

"Certainly."

"Also, would it be all right if I went in your house to have another look around?"

Alice chuckled. "You have so much fun playing private eye."

"Yes, I do."

"You can go in our house any time *[crackle]* —— like, Dan. I believe Maxine still has a key to the place."

"Thanks, Alice."

"Hello?"

"Can you hear me, Alice?"

"Hello? Dan, are *[crackle]* —— there?"

Dan hung up his cell and slipped it back into his pocket. "Lost her," he said.

Red was sipping his room temperature Scotch and staring at the case board. "If this mystery woman was up to no good, then why did she make a point of coming outside and confronting you about the dog crap in the yard, and the smell of your cigar?"

"Good point," Dan replied. "Maybe she *wanted* me to see her ... and remember her."

"Why would a murderer want you to see her? You could identify her later."

"Maybe she's not the killer." Dan stepped forward, picked up the green marker from the tray below the board, and wrote WANTED TO BE SEEN.

"Wanted to be seen," Red read aloud. "So if she didn't kill him the guy, then who did?"

The two men heard a car door slam out front and turned around. Through the glass panel in the front door they could see Rick Carver trudging up the walkway.

73

"Shit!" said Dan. "It's Rick."

"What do we do?" Red asked.

Grab that blanket on the back of the couch and throw it over the case board." Dan met Rick at the front door. "Hey, Rick. What a surprise."

Chief Carver watched over Dan's shoulder as Red adjusted the blanket over the case board. "What's going on here?" he asked.

"Nothing," Red answered.

"Actually, less than that," Dan clarified.

Rick stepped inside the living room. His eyes went to the hole in the couch, and then to the plywood over the broken window. Lastly, he gazed up through the hole in the ceiling. "What did Maxine say about the mess?"

Dan shrugged. "Not much. The new couch comes Friday and the new window comes in tomorrow or the next day."

"Who are you getting to put it in?" Rick asked. "I can give you my guy's number if you want."

"I don't need your guy's number," said Dan. "I'm putting it in myself. I used to be a contractor you know."

"I know," Rick responded. "So do you want my guy's number, or what?"

"No."

"He's got me helping him," Red added.

"Well, if you change your mind," said Rick.

Just then the blanket slid off the case board and landed in a wad on the hardwood floor.

"Not doing anything, huh?" Rick asked. "Looks like you're gathering evidence on a case I told you to stay away from."

"We're just trying to help," said Red.

"No one needs your help," Rick shot back. He took a deep breath, held it for a second, and exhaled slowly.

Red gave Rick a condescending grin. "Now, Rick, I think we both know I have a plaque and citation hanging on the wall behind my bar that states otherwise. You'll recall that we helped your department find a little girl who had been abducted and returned her safely to her family. I think if anyone should be helping you, it should be heroes like me and Dan."

Dan chuckled.

Rick stared at the big man without reaction. Dan and Red waited for Rick to yell, which is what he usually did after Red spoke, but no yelling came. Rick turned and walked to the case board. "What have you got so far?" he asked.

Dan and Red looked at each other with surprise. "Not a helluva lot," replied Dan.

Rick inspected the timeline, as well as the notes Dan had made. "Nothing came back on the victim," Rick remarked, "and being a rental for most of the year, there were prints all over the place," Rick stated.

"Hmm," Dan responded.

"Hmm," Red aped him.

Rick continued. "I phoned the Stewarts—they're on a cruise up in Alaska."

"You don't say," Dan replied.

"Yeah," said Rick, "and Mrs. Stewart says they didn't have the house rented for this week."

"Any sign of forced entry?" Dan asked.

"No," said Rick.

"Most people with any brains at all can break into a house without leaving signs of a break-in," Red said. "If they have the time to think about it, and no one is around."

"In this neighborhood, someone's always around," Dan argued.

"Then why didn't anyone but you see the woman in the green Beamer?" asked Rick.

"Good point," Dan responded.

"Are you getting a list of green BMWs with Florida plates?" asked Red.

"Yes, but as you might guess, there's a lot of them. We'll start local and then widen the perimeter."

"Also, that Beamer might have had phony plates," Red observed.

"And there's that," Rick said.

Dan downed the rest of his tequila and went toward the bar. "Drink, Rick?" he asked.

Rick removed his sunglasses and put them in his shirt pocket. "Yeah, I'm off duty, why not?"

"What'll it be?"

"Whatever you're having."

"You?" Dan asked Red.

"I'm good," Red replied, holding up his glass.

Dan made himself another drink and one for Rick as well. As he did, Rick and Red studied the case board.

"Here ya go," said Dan, handing Rick his drink. Rick took the drink and immediately took a big gulp. He didn't even complain about the lack of ice.

For the next forty-five minutes the men stood in Dan's living room bouncing ideas off each other. Whenever Dan and Red came up with an idea, Rick would calmly explain why it couldn't have happened that way.

Rick placed his empty glass on Dan's end table. "Well, I better get going," he said. "Laura and I are having dinner with the mayor this evening."

"That's gotta be brutal," said Dan.

"Ah, Lyndsay ain't that bad," Rick replied.

Dan walked Rick to the front door and watched as Rick ambled down the sidewalk to his Bronco and drove away. He turned to Red. "What the hell was that?"

"Yeah, right?" said Red. "Who the hell stole our chief of police and put that pod person in his place? He didn't yell at me or call me stupid once the whole time he was here. He didn't even holler at us when he saw the case board."

"And when we came up with ideas, he didn't call them moronic."

"You think he's dying?"

Dan considered this. "Maybe he just found out he *wasn't* dying."

"Maybe he's on drugs."

"Rick, on drugs? I don't think so."

"Maybe they're prescription drugs," Red suggested, "like Zoloft or Prozac."

"I don't know, but something is different. He didn't even seem to mind that he would be spending the evening with the mayor."

Red picked the blanket up off the floor, folded it, and tossed it over the back of the couch, covering the shotgun hole the best he could. "It was nice not being called a moron for a change."

Dan picked up Rick's glass and his own and started for the kitchen. "Yeah, he sure seemed happy."

"Maybe we could get you on something like that."

Dan snapped his head around. "What the fuck is that supposed to mean?"

"Well, you're always kind of in a bad mood … don't ya think?"

"No, ya asshole, I don't think."

"I mean, you know, how you just called me an asshole for no reason. You're kinda mean and always a little grumpy."

"For no reason?" Dan asked. "Maybe I'm always in a bad mood because I have to deal with people like you."

"People like me? Who else?"

Dan began counting on his fingers. "Skip, Mel, Buddy—"

"Buddy? Your dog? You're blaming your attitude on your dog. Wow." Red followed Dan into the kitchen with his own empty glass and placed it in the sink. "Forget I said anything."

"Oh, I usually do."

"That's another dig, right there."

"Shut up, ya moron."

"And another."

The two amateur sleuths went back into the living room and returned their attention to the case board.

"What's next?" asked Red.

"Well, sweetheart," Dan said, in the happiest tone he could muster. "If you would be so kind as to call your friend Garcia over at the DMV and have him get us that same list of green BMWs, that would be awesome."

"I can do that."

"Did I say that pleasant enough for ya?"

"I know it was sarcasm, but yes, that was very nice for a change. Thank you." Red turned and made his way to the front door. "I'll call you tomorrow when I get the list."

"Thank you so much," Dan said. "You are a great friend to have, and so, so, smart."

Red smiled and nodded. "Thank you."

Chapter Nine

Friday afternoon Dan walked into Red's and jumped upon his bar stool. "Tequila, Seven, and lime," he said.

Cindy Leonard was behind the bar. "I understand congratulations are in order," she said, as she made Dan his drink. "I'm so happy for you and Maxine."

"Thanks, Cindy," Dan replied. "Red around?"

"He's in his office." Cindy set Dan's drink in front of him. "You want me to get him?"

"Give it a bit. Let me have the first half of this drink in peace."

The petite blonde chuckled. "That was a beautiful engagement ring."

"Thanks. Where did you see it?"

"Facebook, Instagram, and Snapchat," Cindy replied. "Maybe even Twitter."

Dan shook his head. "That's great." He slid off the stool. "I'll surprise him—wait, he's alone, right?"

"Yup."

"Good. Never know what you might see in there when he doesn't know you're coming in."

Dan rounded the bar and went through the swinging door into the kitchen. Jocko, Red's cook, sat perched on an old wooden stool peeling potatoes.

"Hey, Coast," said Jocko.

"Hey, Jocko," Dan responded.

Dan went through the kitchen and knocked on the solid wooden door with the metal plate that read OFFICE. He knocked three times and turned the doorknob. "Red?"

"Yup," Red replied. "Come on in."

Dan entered the dark, smoky office. Red sat at his desk with his feet up, reading the latest issue of Women's Health. A cigar hung from the corner of the big guy's mouth. The only sound was the grinding and clattering of Red's ancient printer.

"You get that list yet?" Dan asked.

Red pointed at the printer. "It's printing as we speak."

Dan looked at the small stack of computer paper. "How the hell many pages is it?"

"Eight."

"Eight pages? There's that many green BMWs with Florida plates?"

"Well, it would have helped if you knew the plate number ... or even a couple of the numbers."

Dan grimaced. "It's Maxine's fault. If she would have let me get my camera out, I could have gotten a photo of the car, the plate, *and* the un-sub."

Red looked up from his magazine. "Un-sub?" he asked.

"Unknown subject," Dan explained. "They say it all the time on *Criminal Minds*."

"Un-sub. I like it."

Dan sat down in the wooden chair across from his friend. "Women's Health, huh? Interesting," he commented.

"There's a lot of ladies in workout apparel in here," Red responded defensively. He turned the page and then turned the magazine around so Dan could have a look. Dan admired the photograph of a young brunette wearing nothing but a sports bra and a tiny pair of Spandex shorts. The girl was running along a hilly path. In the background was the famous Hollywood sign. "Not bad, eh?" said Red.

"Pretty nice," Dan agreed. "But she's probably not a runner. She's just a model who's pretending she's a runner."

"Why do you always have to spoil my joys in life" Red grumbled. He wet his thumb and turned the page." Here's an interesting article: 'Can Sex Stretch the Vagina?' Says right here a woman's vagina can stretch to accommodate a tampon, a penis, a baby—"

"Stop right there!" Dan shouted. "I don't want to hear about stretched vaginas. I just got engaged, for Chrissakes and Maxine mentioned children for the first time."

For once, Red was speechless.

The printer stopped. Red closed the magazine and tossed it on his desk. "Let's see what we got," he said. He leaned back in his chair, grabbed the paperwork from the printer tray behind him, and handed it to Dan.

Dan flipped through the pages. "Where to start," he said.

"At the top," Red recommended.

"The first one on the list is a guy by the name of Abel Atkins who lives in Walnut Hill. That's almost nine hundred miles from here, so maybe we'll start with the ones here in town."

"But what if the unsub isn't local? Rick said they were starting their search locally. Maybe we should start our search a little farther out."

"I wish I could remember something about the car that would narrow our search."

"Me too." Red leaned forward in his chair and rested his elbows on the desk top. "Close your eyes."

"What?"

"Close your eyes."

"What for?"

"Just do it."

Dan shut his eyes and then opened them again. "You're not gonna throw something at me, are ya?"

"No. Close 'em."

"Dan shut his eyes again.

"Now relax," Red said. "Empty your head."

"Like yours?"

"Shut up, smart-ass. Breathe in through your nose, and exhale through your mouth."

"If I crow like a rooster every time the alarm goes off, I'm gonna be pissed."

"Can't you be serious?"

"No."

"Now, go back to Tuesday morning. What do you see?"

"A dead man in a robe."

"Before that."

"Mailman."

"Mailman?"

"Yeah that goddamn mailman can't seem to match the numbers on the envelops with—"

"Go back to when you first say the Beamer in the driveway."

"Okay."

"Then what?"

"No!" Dan screamed. "No!" He waved his arms in the air. "Stop! Stop! Oh my God!"

"What is it?" Red shouted. "What do you see?"

"The inside of my eyelids, ya jackass," Dan replied. "This isn't gonna work."

"You're an idiot."

"Never said I wasn't."

Red leaned back in his chair. "I wish we knew a real hypnotist."

"It wouldn't work."

"Sure it would. They do it on TV all the time in crime shows."

"This is real life," Dan reminded his pal.

"Wow. It's like I don't even know who you are any more." Red opened the top drawer of his desk and pulled out a phone book. "This is Key West, for Chrissakes. There must be a hypnotist somewhere on this rock." He began flipping through the pages. "H … H … H … Right here. Weird."

"What's weird?" asked Dan.

"There's nothing under hypnotist, but there's two people under hypnotherapy. Is that the same thing?"

Dan shrugged. "Close enough I would imagine."

Red removed his desk phone from its cradle. "Should I give him a call?"

"No."

"Why not?"

"I'm not gonna have some guy I don't know digging around in my head."

"Come on. It shouldn't take long. Where's your sense of adventure? Besides, if we can narrow this list down a bit, it will put us ahead of the game."

"What game?"

"Rick's game. Maybe we can solve this before he does."

Dan thought about it for a second. "Okay, you talked me into it."

"Nice!" Red dialed the number and put it on speaker.

"Hello?" came a man's voice.

"Hi," Red said. "Can I speak to The Amazing Gary please?"

"Speaking."

"Fantastic. Amazing Gary, I was wonder—"

"You can just call me Gary."

"Oh. That just doesn't sound as amazing."

"Sorry."

"Would it be okay if I called you Amazing?" Red asked.

"I guess."

"Amazing, I have a friend who saw a license plate three days ago, but he can't remember any of the numbers on the plate. Is that something you might be able to help us with?"

"I may be able to. Under hypnosis, many subjects are able to recall things in vivid detail that they thought they had forgotten completely."

"Almost like having a photogenic memory."

"Um, yes."

"Would it be possible for you to see us today?"

"Tomorrow would be better. I have an appointment at five, and another at six."

"He can pay you triple."

"Hey!" Dan said.

"Be here at five," said The Amazing Gary.

"Thank you," Red said, and hung up. He looked at Dan. "This is gonna be awesome."

"No, it's gonna be Amazing. I think Awesome is Gary's brother."

"Ha-ha. After you remember the plate number—"

"If I remember the number."

"*When* you remember the number, I'll call Garcia back and *boom* case closed"

"Boom?"

"Bang?"

Dan tossed the list of names back on Red's desk and stood up. "Let's get another drink."

"Should you drink before getting hypnotized?"

"Drinking probably makes it easier to get hypnotized. I would think it opens your mind right up."

"That makes sense." Red stood, and together the two men walked through the kitchen and into the bar. Dan took a seat on his favorite barstool and Red jumped behind the bar to make the drinks. He glanced over his shoulder at the clock. "We have to be there in an hour," he commented.

"Oh, good. We have time for two drinks."

Red chuckled.

"Be where?" Cindy asked.

"Nowhere," Dan replied.

"I'm taking him to get hypnotized," said Red.

"That's fantastic," Cindy said. She sounded a little too excited.

"Why's that fantastic?" Dan asked.

"Well, I had a friend who wanted to quit smoking. She went and got hypnotized and she hasn't had a cigarette in four years."

"I don't smoke," Dan reminded her.

"Yeah, but I'm sure it works the same for drinking."

"That's not why I'm being hypnotized," Dan said angrily.

"Oh, sorry," said Cindy.

Red chuckled. "We're going to see if it will help him remember a license plate number he saw," Red explained.

"Sorry," said Cindy. "I just assumed—"

"Yeah, you just assumed," said Dan.

Red set Dan's drink in front of him. "Here ya go, pal."

Dan continued to glare at Cindy. "Thanks," he said. "And it's *photographic* memory."

"What?" Red asked.

"When you were talking to The Amazing Gary, you said *photogenic* memory. It's photographic."

"You just can't let anything go, can you?"

"Nope."

"You're such a dick."

"Never said I wasn't."

Chapter Ten

Dan pulled his Porsche to the curb in front of a lime green bungalow on Flagler Avenue, between Eleventh and Twelfth streets.

"This must be the place," said Red.

"It's just a regular house," Dan commented.

"What did you expect, a circus tent?"

"I don't know. Something more amazing, I guess."

The two men got out of Dan's car and walked up to the gate in the chain link fence that surrounded the property. A 3x2 sign on a wooden post stood in the front yard. The sign read. THE AMAZING GARY: PALM READING, TAROT READING, AND HYPNOTHERAPY.

"Palm reading?" Dan asked unconvincingly. "Tarot cards? What the Christ have you gotten me into?"

"Open your mind," Red said.

"You mean, open my wallet."

"That too."

"We can pay triple," Dan grumbled.

"It got us an appointment, didn't it?" Red lifted the latch and pushed open the gate. "After you."

Dan went through the gate and walked up to the front door. He knocked three times, then pushed the doorbell.

"Do you think he can contact the dead?" Dan asked.

"We can ask."

The front door opened with a creak that sounded as though Herman Munster had answered the door at 1313 Mockingbird Lane.

"Good afternoon," said a tall, aristocratic gentleman, attired in a shabby purple garment Dan recognized as a smoking jacket. His grayish hair was receding at the temple; a widow's peak descended toward a pair of blue eyes, alight with intelligence and curiosity. The nose was long and noble. The hollow cheeks, Dan observed, were deep enough to plant tomatoes in. He immediately thought of horror movie great Peter Cushing. "How can I help you, gentlemen?" His voice was cultured like Cushing's too.

"I'm Red Baxter, and this is Dan Coast," Red explained. "I called earlier and made an appointment."

The Amazing Gary pulled the door all the way open. "Ah, yes, I've been expecting you."

"And you must be The Amazing Gary," said Red.

"Let's not be so formal. I insist you call me Gary. Please come inside." The elegant seer extended his long, skinny arm with an inviting flourish.

Dan and Red looked at each other for a second before entering. A small part of each of them thought they might never walk out of Gary's house alive—dead maybe, if Gary could turn the living into the walking dead.

Dan went in first, and Red followed. They were standing in the middle of a small living room; about 10x10, Dan estimated, drawing on his former vocation as a contractor. On the floor was red shag carpet that had seen its best days in the early seventies—probably around the same time it was last vacuumed. The walls were papered in a gaudy floral design and reminded Dan of whore houses he'd seen in old Westerns. A small round wooden table sat in the middle of the room; arranged around it were four wooden chairs. Sitting on the table was a crystal ball. Above the table hung an antique brass chandelier. Eerie funeral home music played softly from an unseen speaker. A homemade curtain hung in front of the only doorway to another room. Dan figured the other room was where Gary kept the shoes, underwear, and teeth of his victims.

"Please ... sit," said Gary.

Dan and Red exchanged glances once again before taking their seats. Gary seated himself directly across from Dan, with Red to his left.

"I understand you want to recall the characters on a license plate," said Gary.

"Um, yes," Dan replied.

The Amazing Gary closed his eyes and laid his arms on the table, palms up and fingers extended. "Take my hands," he commanded.

Red reached across the table and placed his hands on top of Gary's.

"Not you," said Gary.

Red pulled back his hands and placed them in his lap.

Dan shook his head as he grasped Gary's hands.

"You're in a lot of pain," Gary said.

"My hemorrhoids are flaring up," Dan joked.

Gary opened his eyes and fixed Dan in an icy stare. "Sir, your locker room humor is most inappropriate."

Well, la-di-da, Dan thought. "Sorry, I didn't mean to interrupt you while you get in tune with the infinite."

Gary ignored the snide *Wizard of Oz* reference and resumed his trance. "You've lost someone close to you."

Dan looked to Red and rolled his eyes.

"Someone you loved very much," Gary continued. He flinched. "There was a car accident."

Dan tried to let go of Gary's hands, but Gary squeezed tighter.

"A dog," said Gary.

The hair on Dan's arms and neck stood up and he felt a chill run up his back. He continued to pull away, but Gary's grip was like a vice.

"I see an A," Garry said. "Alexandra ... or Alexis—"

Dan yanked his hands back, finally breaking free of Gary's clutches. He stood and backed away from the table. His chair flipped over backwards. "You sick fuck!" Dan shouted. "What the Christ is wrong with you?"

Red stood and Gary grabbed his arm.

"Wait—give him a second," Gary said in his dulcet voice.

Dan's hands trembled as he rubbed his eyes and ran his fingers through his hair. He felt as though ice water was running through his veins.

"That's not what we came here for," Red said angrily.

Gary continued to stare at Dan. "That's what *he* came here for."

"Let's go," Dan said, as he turned toward the front door.

"What about the license plate?" Red asked.

"Fuck the license plate," Dan shot back. He placed his hand on the doorknob.

"Are you sure you want to leave?" Gary asked.

Dan paused.

"Let's just get the plate number and we'll leave," Red said.

Dan stood perfectly still for a few seconds wondering what he should do. He turned back and pointed his index finger at Gary. "No more bullshit, Gary, or I'll shove that crystal ball so far up your ass all you'll see is a dark and shitty future."

The bobbing of Gary's prominent Adam's apple as he gulped indicated he understood.

Dan walked slowly back to the table, the heat returning to his body. He lowered himself back down across from Gary.

Gary removed a shiny silver ballpoint pen from his shirt pocket and held it in his fingertips. "I want you to focus on this pen," he said. He moved the pen slowly from right to left and back again. The ink tip pointed at the table with the clicker pointing at the ceiling. Each time the pen moved directly under the chandelier there was a quick flash of light. "Remember back to the morning you saw the car." Gary continued to move the pen. Dan waited for the flash with each pass. "Where was the car parked?"

"My neighbor's driveway," Dan replied.

"What color was the car?"

"Green." Dan could feel himself relax as Gary spoke. He wondered if he was being hypnotized. He wondered if that were something someone would wonder if they were in deed hypnotized.

"Look down at the license plate," said Gary. "What state do you see?"

"Florida."

"Look at the plate number. Tell me the plate number, Dan."

"I can't—"

"You're looking right at the number, Dan. It's plain as day. What is it?"

"B ... C ... H ... 5436."

Red yanked the pen out of Gary's hand and quickly wrote the number on the palm of his hand.

Gary snapped his fingers. "And you're back!" he cried.

"I never left," said Dan.

Red held up his hand to show Dan the numbers. "You knew the characters."

"I know," Dan replied. "I remember everything. I wasn't hypnotized."

"It's not like on television," Gary offered.

Dan stood and reached for his money clip. "How much?"

"Two hundred," Gary answered.

Dan counted out the money and tossed it on the table in front of Gary. "Come on."

"Dan," Gary said, as the two men reached the door.

Dan didn't turn around. "What?"

"She's happy you moved down here."

"Fuck you," Dan said, and walked out the door.

When Dan and Red got back into the car and shut the doors, Dan's cell phone rang. "Hello?" Dan answered.

"What's up?" Maxine asked.

"Not much," Dan replied. "Just leaving the hypnotist."

"Hypnotist?" Maxine asked. "You went to a hypnotist?"

"It was Red's idea."

"That's great," said Maxine. "Do you still feel like you need a drink?"

"What the Christ!" said Dan. "That's not why I went. I'll explain it to you later."

"Okay. Just checking in, and I wanted to let you know I was going to do a double shift, so I won't be home until tomorrow morning."

"Okay, thanks."

"Love you."

"Back at ya," Dan replied. He hung up his cell and tossed it into the console. He started the car, put it in gear, and pulled away from the curb.

"Your future will be dark and shitty," Red said with a chuckled. "That was a good one."

"Yeah," Dan said.

"You okay?" Red asked, as they drove down Flagler Avenue.

"Nothing a bottle of tequila won't cure."

Chapter Eleven

"Hey," said Bev. She nudged Dan's arm. "Hey. You alive?"

Dan groaned as he opened his eyes. He was staring down through the ropes of his hammock at an empty tequila bottle that lay on the ground beneath him. "What's the matter?" he asked.

"Did you sleep out here all night?" asked Bev.

Dan lifted his throbbing head. "Aw shit. What time is it?"

"Almost seven."

"Christ, I'm stupid." Dan sat up in the hammock; his feet dangled over the edge. "Maxine gets off work at seven."

"Then I would suggest you get your drunken ass in the house and get cleaned up."

"Good idea." Dan stood and the entire yard spun around him. "Crap, crap, crap."

"You get in the shower and get changed, I'll make you some coffee."

"Thanks."

Bev turned up her nose. "And brush your teeth for God's sake."

Bev watched as Dan staggered up the gravel path to the back door. When he was inside, she bent over, picked up the empty tequila bottle, and tossed it into an overgrown bougainvillea at the edge of the yard. She looked around the yard for any other evidence of her neighbor's stupidity. When she was satisfied there wasn't any, she went inside to make him a cup of coffee.

Bev was leaning up against the countertop, in front of the sink, when Dan entered the kitchen after his speedy shower. He was dressed in a clean pair of tan cargo shorts, and a black T-shirt. On his feet were one of his favorite pairs of flip-flops—the Bob Marley ones with the burlap insole.

"You want to tell me about it?" Bev asked, as she picked up a mug and filled it with coffee. She handed the mug to Dan.

"Tell you about what?" Dan asked.

"Something must be bothering you. I haven't seen you like that in quite some time."

"It's nothing." Dan blew into the cup and took a sip.

"It must be something," Bev argued. "Having second thoughts about proposing?"

"No, it's not that." Dan lifted his hot mug and pressed it against his aching forehead.

Bev turned, opened the cupboard, and took out an aspirin bottle. She counted out six aspirins and handed them to the hurting lug. Dan took the tablets from her and tossed them to the back of his throat. He washed them down with a gulp of coffee. "Jesus, that's hot."

"You know you can talk to me about anything, Dan," said Bev.

"I know."

Two pieces of toast Bev had put in the toaster popped up. She grabbed them and held them out to Dan. "Here, choke these down. It'll settle your stomach."

Dan took the toast and bit off a small piece of the corner of one of the slices. "Red and I went to a hypnotist yesterday afternoon."

"To help you with your drinking?" Bev asked.

"No," Dan groaned. "Not to help me with my drinking."

"I just assumed—"

Dan took another bite of the toast. "I know what you assumed, but we went there to see if I could remember the plate number of the Beamer that was parked in the Stewart's driveway the other morning." Dan paused, turned, and stared out the back screen door over his lawn and out to the beach. A small aluminum motor boat zipped by about fifty yards offshore. Dan watched the sleek runabout until it was out of sight.

"Did something happen at the hypnotist?" Bev asked.

Dan took a deep breath. "The guy grabbed my hands and said that he could see—"

"Honey, I'm home," Maxine sang out as she walked through the front door.

"We'll talk about it later," Dan whispered.

"Morning, Bev," said Maxine, when she entered the kitchen. She was carrying the morning's edition of the Key West Citizen in her hand. She walked to Dan and kissed him on the lips, then tossed the paper on the countertop. "I figured you would still be in bed."

"No," Dan said. "I've been up for a while."

"Toast for breakfast?" Maxine asked.

"Yup," Dan replied. "You want a cup of coffee?"

"No thanks. I'm going to put on my pajamas and get a few hours of sleep, but first I want to hear about your trip to the hypnotist."

"I'd like to hear about that too," said Bev. She turned and took a coffee cup out of the cupboard for herself.

Dan shoved the last of one of the slices of toast into his mouth. "Not much to tell," he responded, with his mouth full.

"Well, first," said Maxine, "why did you go to a hypnotist?"

"To see if I could remember the plate number of the BMW next door."

"And did you?" asked Bev.

"Yes."

"What was it?" Maxine asked.

"I don't remember it now," Dan explained. "Red wrote it down."

"I bet that made Chief Carver happy," said Maxine.

"Um ... well—"

"You didn't tell him," Bev surmised.

"No."

"You're not going to tell him, are you?" asked Maxine.

"No."

"Why not?" asked Bev.

"Because Red and I want to solve this case."

"Rick told you to stay out of it."

"He always says that."

"But you don't think he means it."

"No. It's just a formality."

"A formality?" Bev asked.

"Yeah," said Dan. "He has to say that so if anything bad happens, it's not his or the departments fault."

"You really believe that?" Maxine asked.

"Of course. Who wouldn't want my help?"

"It's amazing how your mind works."

"Thank you," said Dan.

"I don't think she meant that as a compliment," Bev said.

"What other way could she mean it?" Dan asked.

Maxine leaned in for another kiss. "You have issues," she said. She turned around and headed for the hallway. "I'm going to bed. Don't get yourself in any trouble please."

After Bev heard the bedroom door shut she turned to Dan. "You want to talk about it now?"

"I'd rather not," Dan replied.

"You know where I am if you do." Bev gave Dan a hug and a kiss on the cheek.

Dan nodded his head. "Thanks."

Bev turned and walked to the back door. "I'm taking this coffee with me." She went out the door and down the back steps.

Dan refilled his coffee cup, grabbed the newspaper, and he too went out the backdoor. He walked down the gravel path to the fire pit and took a seat in one of the Adirondack chairs. He sat his coffee cup on the ground next to his chair and unfolded the paper. UNIDENTIFIED MAN FOUND DEAD IN LOCAL RENTAL PROPERTY, the headline read. *Boring*, he thought, and turned to the funnies to see what Beetle Bailey was up to.

Chapter Twelve

Dan puttered around the house and watched some television as quietly as he could while Maxine slept. Around noon his boredom had reached maximum capacity and he decided to drive over to Red's Bar and Grill for lunch.

On his way to Red's, Dan swung by the Key West Cigar Club and grabbed a couple Arturo Fuente's and a couple Rocky Patels. He bit the tip off one of the Fuente's and lit it while standing on the concrete patio in front of the cigar shop. He took a long drag as he gazed up Duval Street one way, and down the other. He opened his mouth a little and let the aromatic smoke find its way out while inhaling ever so gently through his nose. The cigar tasted good and smelled great as well. Dan blew out the remainder of the smoke and took a seat in one of the four metal chairs in front of the picture window, underneath the blue and white striped canvas awning. He stretched his legs out in front of him and crossed his legs at the ankles.

Dan sat there and watched the tourists stroll by. Some carried ice cream cones, and others carried plastic cups filled with beer, pina coladas, margaritas, or whatever else tourists drank as they strolled along.

It wasn't too many years earlier that Dan himself was a tourist, walking the streets of Key West with a drink in his hand thinking, *Is this legal*? He remembered walking along hand in hand with his wife, Alex. He remembered it like it was yesterday. He could recall almost every step. He knew which souvenir shops they entered, which art galleries they visited, and every purchase they made. He thought about an 8x10 watercolor print of the funky yellow facade of Captain Tony's Saloon that Alex wanted. He remembered mentally counting the contents of his wallet wondering if they could afford it. They probably couldn't, but Dan bought it for her any way. That print now stored in a plastic tote in Dan's parents' basement.

Dan shook his head, bringing himself back to the present. He had found himself thinking of the past a lot more since his visit to The Amazing Gary. *Amazing, my ass*, Dan thought.

After a few more minutes, Dan climbed out of his chair and walked down the steps to the sidewalk. He left his Porsche where it was parked, and walked the two blocks to Captain Tony's for a margarita.

Dan walked along the red brick sidewalk to the familiar yellow building with black shutters. Captain Tony's was a tourist Mecca with a rich and fascinating history dating to the 1850s. In its many incarnations the building had housed, among other things, a bordello, a morgue, and even a cigar factory; Dan thought that fact was particularly cool. When Hemingway and his fishing buddies were regulars, it was the original Sloppy Joe's. In the 1980s, when the place was refurbished, bones were discovered underneath the floorboards, as well as the gravestone of a young woman named Elvira Edmunds. The marker was preserved and, ensconced beside the pool table, was now a macabre conversation piece.

Dan hopped up the step and went in through the doors that lead to the souvenir shop side of Captain Tony's bar. In another macabre touch, the bar was built around the hanging tree, where in the 1800s, several pirates were strung up for their dastardly deeds.

The joint had long been a favorite watering hole of artists, writers, actors, and other artistic types. According to tradition, whenever a big-time celebrity visited, a barstool was christened in his or her name. Dan took a seat on the stool bearing Dan Akroyd's name. He would have plopped his ass on Jimmy Buffett's stool, but it was occupied.

"What can I get for ya, pal?" asked the bartender cordially.

"Two margaritas," Dan replied. "On the rocks."

The bartender made the drinks. He placed them both in front of Dan and Dan placed a twenty next to the plastic cups. Dan sipped one of the drinks and then leaned his forearms against the bar. He took a deep breath and let it out slowly. A thin young man with a ponytail sat on a stool near the entrance and sang "Carefree Highway" as he strummed an acoustic guitar.

"Goddamn you, Amazing Gary," Dan whispered. He glanced down at the empty barstool next to him, and slid the other margarita over in front of it.

"Meeting someone here?" the bartender asked, just trying to be friendly.

"Yeah," Dan said.

"Girlfriend?"

"No, just an angel I used to know."

The young bartender gave Dan an odd look but left it at that.

Dan sat there and nursed his drink, and listened to a few more songs. When the drink was gone he got up and walked to the door, tipping the young musician on his way out. Once outside he took one last long drag on his cigar and dropped it at his feet. He crushed it under his flip-flop, picked it back up, and tossed it into a curbside trash can.

Dan looked up at the huge stuffed jewfish, said to have been caught by Captain Tony Terracino himself, mounted over the bar's sign. It was another Captain Tony's tradition for tourists to try to toss a quarter into the jewfish's gaping mouth; if it went in, legend said, good luck would follow you after you departed the island. Of course, both Dan and Alex had given it a shot. Dan's quarter was on the money. Alex's was not. Before starting back down Greene Street, Dan looked back over his shoulder, through the doorway, and into the bar, at the still-full margarita he had left there.

Chapter Thirteen

Dan walked through the swinging double doors and into the darkness of Red's Bar and Grill. He stood at the door for a second and pulled off his Ray Bans to let his eyes adjust.

"Hey, pal," Red called out from behind the bar.

Dan walked across the room and tossed one of the Fuentes onto the bar top. "Tequila, Seven and lime," he said.

"That for me?" Red asked.

"I don't see anyone else here," said Dan.

"What's your problem?" Red grabbed a rocks glass and filled it with ice.

"I don't have a problem."

Red added a shot of tequila and topped off the glass with 7UP. "Is it about The Amazing Gary bringing up your wife?" he asked. "Sorry about that." He slid the drink across the bar to his friend.

"No," Dan replied. "I never gave that a second thought. I forgot all about it."

"That's good. I have to admit, that had me a little worried."

"Oh yeah? Why's that?" Dan picked up his drink and downed half of it in the first gulp.

"Because of that," said Red. "I remember what you were like before Maxine came along."

Dan downed the remainder of his drink and slid the empty glass back across the bar. "Nothing to worry about. I'm fine."

"Mm-hmm." Red made the next drink. "A little slower this time, please."

"You ain't my mother."

"No, but kind of like a brother."

"I had a brother once. No need for another." Dan sipped this time. "Garcia run that plate?"

"He should be getting back to me any time now."

Dan smiled. "Rick's gonna be pissed when we find the owner of that car before him."

"There's that pretty smile," Red said.

"Frig you."

"You hungry?"

"Yeah."

"Fish sandwich and fries?"

"Yeah."

Red side stepped to the kitchen door and pushed it open a couple inches. "Jocko!"

"What!" Jocko shouted back.

"Fish sandwich and fries!"

"Got it!"

Red let the door shut and stepped back up to the bar. "Maxine working?" he asked.

"Sleeping."

Red's cell phone rang; he turned and answered the bar phone. "Red's Bar and Grill," he announced. "Hello?"

The cell rang again.

"It's your cell phone, ya moron."

Red set the phone back in its cradle and went for his cell.

"Why do you have the same ringer on both your phones?" Dan asked.

"Because I just like my cell sound like an old-fashioned phone," Red answered.

"That's weird."

"Said the pot to the kettle. Hello? Hey, Garcia." Red put his hand over the mic. "It's Garcia."

"Gee, thanks for the newsflash," Dan said.

"Okay, hold on." Red searched the bar for a pen and piece of paper. "I need a pen."

"So?" said Dan.

"Find me one."

"Where?"

"I don't know." Red shook his head. "Jocko!"

"What?"

"I need a pen!"

"Good for you!"

Dan chuckled.

"Hold on, Garcia. I'm surrounded by idiots." Red placed his cell phone on the bar, turned, and ran through the kitchen door.

Dan reached over and picked up the pen than lay behind the napkin holder. He grabbed Red's cell. "Hey, Garcia, it's Coast. Whaddaya got for us?"

Dan began writing on a napkin. "Okay … got it … thanks." Dan hung up the cell and put it back where he got it.

Red ran back through the door with a pen. "Got one, dick head." He picked up his phone. "Go ahead." He grabbed a napkin and readied himself to take notes. "Garcia? Hello?" Red pulled the phone away from his ear. "He hung up."

"Crap," said Dan. "Why didn't you just take the phone with you?"

"I don't know."

"You want me to tell you why?"

"Shut up. Now we gotta wait for him to call us back."

Dan showed Red his napkin. "Or we could just use this information."

"Where did you get that from?"

"From Garcia while you were looking for a pen."

"Where did you get a pen?'

"Right here behind the napkin holder. Why, did you want to use it?"

"What is wrong with you?"

"My mother's dying wor—"

"Yeah, yeah, your mother's dying words. Your mother's not dead. Blah, blah, blah."

Dan looked down at the napkin as his friend rambled on. "According to this, those plates didn't come from a green BMW."

"What did they come from?" Red poured himself a shot of Scotch and downed it.

"Slow down there, drunky," said Dan.

"I need a drink. You drive me nuts. Ya make me run around looking for a pen when there's one sit—"

"You still on that?"

"Where did the plates come from?" Red shot back.

"They came off a blue 2012 Honda Civic owned by a man named Corky Maddigan."

"Corky?" Red asked surprised.

"That's what it says. Corky Maddigan, 811 McGee Road, Bonifay, Florida."

"Ya think his parents named him Corky?"

"Someone must have named him Corky."

"Strange."

"Where the hell's Bonifay?" Dan asked.

"I have no idea," Red replied.

Dan pulled out his cell phone and searched for Bonifay, Florida on Google Maps. "It's way up north, about an eleven-hour drive." Dan downed the rest of his drink and slid off the back of his stool. "Better get going."

"Going where?"

"To Bonifay, to speak to Corky."

"You just said it was an eleven hour drive."

"Probably twelve with pee stops and food breaks."

"I'm not driving all the way up there just to talk to some guy who got his license plates stolen."

"Come on, it'll be fun. We haven't taken a road trip in a long time."

"We've never taken a road trip," Red argued.

"Well, that is a long time."

Red looked up at the wall behind him at the clock. "It's almost two o'clock. We won't get there until after one in the morning."

"Come on," Dan said. "We'll pack a bag and stop somewhere tonight and sleep. Drive the rest of the way in the morning."

Red moaned. "Now we're packing a bag," he said with a sigh. "I'm tryin' to run a business here."

Dan looked around at the empty room. "I'm the only one here."

"God, I hate you!"

"You do not."

"Let me call Cindy and see if she can come in early."

"You need a pen?" Dan asked.

"Shut up."

Chapter Fourteen

Dan and Red swung by Red's house so Red could pack a few things in a bag for their trip, and then they headed over to Dan's place. Red waited in the Porsche while Dan ran inside.

Dan could hear the shower running and quickly went into the bedroom. He grabbed a small backpack out of the closet and tossed it on the bed. He opened his dresser drawer, grabbed two pairs of underwear, a pair of tan cargo shorts, and two T-shirts. He went back to the closet and grabbed two short-sleeved bowling shirts, turned, and stuffed them into the bag.

The shower shut off; Dan froze for a second. He bent over and picked up a pair of flip-flops and his favorite pair of Margaritaville slip-ons and jammed them into the front zippered pocket of the backpack.

Dan got to the bathroom door just as Maxine, clad in only a towel, opened it.

"Jesus!" she screamed. "I didn't know you were here."

"I am," Dan replied.

Maxine glanced down at the backpack in Dan's hand. "What's going on?" she asked.

"I, uh … I have to take a quick trip up to Bonifay."

"Bonifay? What is that, a grocery store or something? Why do you need a bag?"

"No, it's a small town about eleven hours north of here."

"What?"

"What … what?"

"What do you need to go up there for?"

"A case Red and I are working on."

"I didn't know you were working on a case," said Maxine. "This wouldn't be about the dead guy next door, would it?"

"Kinda."

"Either it is, or it isn't."

"It is."

"Didn't Rick tell you to keep your nose out of it?"

"He did."

Maxine knew when she was licked. "How long are you going to be gone?" she sighed.

"Sunday afternoon the latest."

"What about Stacy's art show?"

"Oh crap," said Dan. "Is that tomorrow?"

"You know it's tomorrow."

Dan pulled his money clip out of his front pocket. "I'll tell you what." He counted out three one hundred-dollar bills. "You take this and buy whatever you want. Tell her I'm sorry for missing it."

"We were supposed to take Mel with us."

"Well now the two of you can have some bonding time." Dan kissed Maxine on the lips. "Thanks for being so understanding."

"Yeah."

"Oh, and don't say anything to Rick about us going up there."

"He's going to be at the art show. What should I tell him?"

"Just make something up. Something believable."

"I'll tell him I killed you and buried you in the backyard. He should believe that."

"He probably wouldn't even arrest you." Dan grabbed his toothbrush and headed for the door.

"Love you!" Maxine called out.

"Back at ya!" Dan hollered.

As Dan walked down the front steps, Skip Stoner pulled up in his Volkswagen Thing. Dan nodded crisply at Red and quickly tossed his backpack into the backseat of the Porsche.

"Yo, dudes!" Skip hollered. The Thing sputtered to a stop. The tall, skinny man-child jumped up on his seat and leapt over the passenger side door, his size eleven Vans hitting the ground with a whoomph. "What do you hombres got goin' on today?"

117

"Nothing," Dan replied.

"What's in the bag, Dan the Man?" Skip asked.

"What bag?" Dan asked.

"The one you just lofted into the car, dude."

"Oh, that bag."

Skip craned his neck to see into Dan's backseat. "You gotta bag there too, Red Man?" he asked.

"Uh, yeah," was Red's reply.

"You guys goin' on an excursion, or something?" Skip's face fell when he realized he hadn't been invited.

"Yeah," said Dan. "We're running up to Bonifay."

"That a clothing store, or something?" Skip asked.

"It's a little town up north," Red said.

"When ya coming back?" Skip asked.

"Sunday, the latest," Dan replied.

"I got the next three days off," Skip said. He stared at the ground and kicked a small stone. "Probably be pretty boring around here."

Dan and Red looked at each other and then back at their pouting friend.

"You want to go with us, Skip?" Dan asked.

Skip looked up; his face beamed with joy. "I thought you'd never ask, Dan the Man."

"Run home and pack," said Red.

"Don't need to, amigo. I keep a go-bag in the Thing at all times."

"Get it and let's go," said Dan.

Skip walked back to his car and pulled the keys out of the ignition. He paused. "Wait. Just throw you guys's stuff in my trunk. We'll take the Thing," he said, popping the trunk.

Red opened his door and climbed out.

"Stay in the car," Dan ordered. "We're taking my car."

"There's more room in mine," Skip argued. "Come on Red Man."

"Stay where you are, Red."

"We might as well just take his car," said Red. He climbed out of the Porsche and shut the door.

"What the Christ?" said Dan. He and Red grabbed their backpacks and threw them into Skip's trunk. "I'm riding shotgun."

Dan glanced into the trunk at the black, four-foot-long duffle bag. "That's your go bag?" he asked.

"Sure is," Skip said proudly. "Ain't she a beaut? It's made out of military-grade Kevlar."

"What do you got in there?" Red asked.

"Everything I need," Skip replied, and slammed the trunk.

"Everything he needs," Dan grumbled, and climbed into the passenger seat.

When everyone was in the car, Skip started the engine. "Please remain seated throughout the entire ride. Keep your arms, legs, and nutsacks inside the car at all times. Remember to hold on tightly to any personal belongings you might have with you—that includes your nutsacks—and as always, enjoy the ride." Skip put the car in drive, and jumped on the gas.

"I've only been in this car for thirty seconds," Dan said, "and I've already heard the word nutsacks two too many times."

"Nutsack!" Red hollered.

Chapter Fifteen

It was a little after eight and the trio was headed north on US-27.

"There's a motel right up here," Dan said. "Just pull in."

"Yeah, I'm pretty tired too," Red agreed.

"You got it, Dan the Man," said Skip, and veered off the road into the parking lot of the State Motel. "Look at that, a diner right in the parking lot. What more could you ask for?"

"A room without bed bugs," Dan replied.

The State Motel was an orange, one-story, cinder block building in the shape of a horseshoe. The R-Place Eatery—a red brick building—sat smack dab in the middle of the parking lot.

Skip parked his vehicle at the south end of the building, in front of the door labeled, OFFICE.

121

The three men piled out of the car and headed for the door. "The rooms probably only have two double beds," Skip commented. "So two of us will have to sleep together."

"Well I know I'm sleeping with you, Skip," said Dan. He pulled open the office door.

"Seriously, dude?" asked Skip.

"No, ya moron," Dan replied. "I'm getting my own room. You two do whatever you want."

"What about me?" Red asked.

"What about you?" asked Dan.

"I can't sleep in your room? This trip was your idea, and now I have to pay for my own room?"

"I'll go halves with you, Red Man," said Skip.

"Thanks, Skip," Red said.

"No problemo."

Dan walked up to the desk and said, "Excuse me, I need a room."

The chubby man, who looked a little too much like John Wayne Gacey for Dan's comfort, glanced up from his *Boys' Life* magazine. "All y'all in one room?" he asked.

"I want my own room," Dan answered.

Red tapped the service bell a couple times.

"Don't do that," the desk clerk said.

"Sorry, Red replied.

"Sixty-four dollars," said the desk clerk.

Dan pulled out his money clip. "I'll pay for both rooms," he said.

"Thanks, Dan the Man," said Skip.

"The pool open?" asked Red.

"Yeah," said the clerk.

Dan paid, got their room keys, and walked out of the office. He handed one of the keys to Red. "You're in seven," he said.

"What are you in?" asked Red.

"Eight."

"I'm gonna put on my swim trunks and jump into that pool to cool off, then we'll get something to eat."

"Roger that," said Skip. He looked at his Timex. "We'll meet back here in twenty."

Dan twirled his key ring around his index finger as he walked along. The three men stopped at the back of Skip's car and grabbed their bags. Skip and Red went into their room, and Dan went into his.

Dan closed his door behind him and dropped his pack on the floor. He grabbed the remote and turned on the TV. The screen told him to press A for cable, and B for adult films; Dan pressed A, and sat down on the bed. He pulled out his cell phone and texted Maxine.

We just got to our motel. Some fleabag for 64 bucks a night. I'll probably have head lice, bed bugs, scabies, and ringworm next time you see me. Going to grab something to eat in a bit. Text you tomorrow.

Dan Knew Maxine was still at work and probably wouldn't text him back until after eleven. He swung his legs up on the bed and dropped his cell phone on the bed next to him. He began flipping through the stations. Two minutes later there was a knock at the door.

"Go away," Dan said.

"I got booze," Skip called out.

"Come on in," Dan said.

Skip opened the door and showed Dan the bottle of tequila he was holding in one hand, and the two-liter bottle of 7UP he held in the other. Squeezed between his forearm and ribs was an old plastic ice bucket.

"Well, if it isn't my best friend, Skip," Dan announced.

Skip grinned. "Thanks, Dan the Man."

"I was talking about the tequila."

"Oh."

"Close the door, you're letting in the mosquitos."

Skip kicked the door shut with the heel of his foot and walked to the small round table in the corner of the room. He set the tequila, ice bucket, and two liter bottle on the table. "Can I make you a drink, sir?" he asked.

"That would be fantastic," Dan replied. "All we need is a—"

Skip pulled a lime from the side pocket of his baggies. "*Wah-lah!* I said I brought everything I needed in my go-bag, broham."

"Your pockets are clean, right?" Dan said. "That lime's been awful close to your nutsack."

"Bro! The Skipster believes that cleanliness is next godliness."

"I bet," Dan mumbled.

Skip filled a plastic cup with ice, added some tequila, and topped it off with 7UP. He reached back into his pocket and pulled out a pocket knife. He sliced the lime into pieces and dropped one into Dan's cup. "Here ya go," he announced.

Dan took the cup and sipped the drink. "Perfect."

"Did you expect anything less?"

"Of course I did," Dan replied. "Where's Red?"

"He put on his board shorts and walked down to the pool," Skip replied, as he made himself a drink. He took a seat in one of the two metal chairs that sat around the table. "What are we watchin'?" He put his feet up on the table and slouched down in the chair.

Dan continued to surf through the channels. "Nothing on," he said. "Look on your cell phone and see what there is to eat around here."

"On it," Skip said, reaching into his pocket.

Dan paused for a minute on a first season rerun of M*A*S*H.

"There's a Wendy's down the street," said Skip.

"Red'll like that," said Dan.

"There's also a Zaxby's."

"I don't feel like getting the shits. What else?"

"They got a BBQ joint down the street."

"I'll be burping all night."

"There's Manny's Original Chop Shop right here across the street, a Dairy Queen, and a McDonald's. That's pretty much it."

"The Chop Shop sounds good."

"Then Manny's it is."

The door swung open, and Red stood in the doorway in his board shorts. His belly hung over the drawstring. He had a pissy look on his face.

"How was the water, Red Man?" Skip asked.

"There wasn't any," Red replied.

Dan laughed. "There wasn't any?"

"No. The damn pool was empty. Didn't the guy at the desk say it was open?"

"Sure did," said Skip.

"The only thing open was the gate," Red complained.

"Maybe that's what he meant," Dan offered.

"On a more enjoyable note," said Red, "there's a Wendy's right down the street."

"We're eating across the street at Manny's," said Skip.

"Says who?" asked Red.

"Says me and Skip," Dan replied.

"Can we at least go there and get a Frosty afterward?"

"Sure," said Dan. "Get dressed."

"I'll just throw on a T-shirt," said Red.

"And pants," Dan added.

"I'm wearing board shorts."

"No you're not."

"Why? Skip's wearing board shorts."

"Skip's over ten years younger than you and over forty pounds lighter. He looks like he's supposed to be wearing board shorts."

"Thanks, bro," Skip said with a grin.

Red looked down at his board shorts and flip-flops. "What do I look like?"

"A fat old man who's running to Walmart at two in the morning for hemorrhoid cream."

Red glared at his friend. "What would that even look like?"

"There's a mirror right over there," Dan said, pointing across the room.

Red spun around and started out the door. "You're a dickhead!"

"Never said I wasn't."

Skip chuckled. "Hemorrhoid cream," he repeated.

Dan and Skip drank their drinks and stared at the TV while they waited for Red to get dressed. The credits scrolled by as "Suicide Is Painless" played, and suddenly there was a loud thump against the other side of Dan's wall. Skip and Dan both flinched.

"What the hell was that?" Skip asked.

"Sounds like Red is a little pissed about the fashion review I gave him."

"That's not our room," said Skip. He pointed in the opposite direction. "We're over there." He got up and walked across the room and put his ear to the wall.

"Can you hear anything?" Dan asked.

"Sounds like someone is arguing," Skip answered.

"What are they arguing about?"

"*Shhh!*"

Dan walked over to put his own ear against the wall. Just as he did there was a thud; it was louder than the thump. The two men jumped back away from the wall.

"Sounded like a dude yelling at his lady," said Skip. "I'm gonna go over there and see if everything is okay."

"Maybe you better stay out of it," Dan suggested.

"Whoa, Dan the Man!" Skip argued. "There could be a damsel in distress." He turned and headed for the door; Dan followed him. When Skip pulled open the door, Red was standing there.

"Hey," Red said. "Leaving without me?"

"No," Dan answered in a sarcastic tone, "we're going next door to rescue a damsel in distress."

"I'm in," said Red.

"That's the spirit, Red Man," said Skip, clapping Red on the back.

The three men walked to the room next door, and Skip knocked.

"Just keep your mouth shut," said a guy inside the room. No one answered him.

Skip gave the door a couple more raps. "Hello?" he called out.

The door opened slowly and a man in his early twenties asked, "Can I help you?" His eyes darted from Dan to Red and back to Skip.

"Is everything okay over here, dude?" Skip asked. He tried to look past the young man into the room.

"Yeah, everything is fine," said the young man.

"We thought we heard some arguing," said Skip.

"Nope. Everything is good." The guy started to close the door but Skip stuck his foot in the doorway. The guy pushed a little harder.

"Who's in there with you?" Skip asked.

"None of your business. Who are you?"

Red walked around Skip and shoved the door open almost knocking the kid over. "Neighborhood watch, asshole," he said. "Get out of the way."

"What the Christ?" Dan mumbled.

The three men walked into the room. Sitting on the king-sized bed was a redhead, about the same age as the young man. She had a black eye, and there was a small cut over her top lip. She had been crying.

The young man turned and started toward his girlfriend. Dan grabbed him by the back of his collar. "Hold on, Sparky," he said.

"Are you okay?" Skip asked the young girl.

The girl, who was wearing red and white checkered pajama bottoms and a men's white T-shirt, nodded her head yes.

"Are you sure about that?" Skip walked toward her. "How'd you get that shiner?"

The girl turned her head away.

"Her dad did that," said Sparky.

Skip knelt down in front of her. "What's your name?"

"Marilyn," said Sparky.

Red turned and pointed his finger at Sparky. "Don't speak again unless you're spoken to," he warned. "He looked at the girl and asked gently, "Your name's Marilyn?"

"Yes."

"Is he telling the truth, Marilyn?" Skip asked. "Did your father do this to you?"

"Yes."

"Where is your father now?"

"West Palm," she said quietly.

"Does he know where you are?"

"No." Marilyn continued to stare at the dingy, dog shit brown shag carpet.

As Skip talked, Red walked around the room checking the place out. There were two small pink suitcases on the floor at the foot of the bed, and a blue backpack hanging over the back of a metal chair. He peeked into the bathroom. There were no personal items on the sink counter.

"How old are you?" Skip asked.

"Twenty-two," Marilyn replied.

"What's your father's name?"

Marilyn just shook her head no.

Skip looked back at the young man. "What's your name?"

"Steve," said the kid. "Steve Foster."

"Who's her father?"

"He's nobody. Just a guy."

"This guy have a name?" Dan asked.

"Jim," Steve replied. "Jim Martin."

Red walked back over near Dan and Steve. Dan had let go of the boy's collar, but Steve remained where he was.

"When did the two of you check in?" Red asked.

"About three hours ago," Steve answered.

Skip returned his attention to Marilyn. "Is there anything we can do?" he asked. "Is there anything you need, or anyone you want us to call?"

Marilyn shook her head again. "No, thank you. We'll be fine."

Skip looked over his shoulder at Dan. Dan shrugged. Skip put his hand on the young girl's knee. "We're gonna go grab something to eat, then we'll be right next door if you need anything. Just pound on that wall."

"Thank you."

"Have you eaten?"

"Yes."

"When?"

"About two hours ago, at the Wendy's down the street."

"Aw, man," said Red.

Dan shot him a look. He side-stepped to a mirrored dresser. "This your cell phone, Marilyn?" he asked.

"Yes," she replied.

Dan picked the phone up off the dresser, tapped the screen a few times, and dialed his own cell number. His phone rang and he placed Marilyn's phone back on the dresser. He answered his phone and hung up. "My number's in your call log. Call if you need anything."

Skip stood and started for the door. He stopped when he got to Steve. "We'll be back to check on her after we eat, Steve. If there's a mark on her that isn't there now, they'll find you at the bottom of that swimming pool in the morning."

"There's no water in that pool," Red reminded him.

"I know," said Skip.

Chapter Sixteen

The three men walked across the six lanes of traffic to Manny's Original Chop Shop.

"This place is packed," said Red, as they crossed the parking lot.

"Noisy too," Dan commented.

Manny's eaves, as well as the gable ends of the building, were lit up in yellow and red neon. A sign on the front of the building, bordered in green neon, spelled out Manny's in big, yellow, block letters. Loud country music played on exterior speakers.

"How y'all doin' this evening?" said the young girl behind the hostess podium.

"Wonderful," said Dan.

"Three?"

"Yut."

"It's gonna be about twenty-five minutes." The young girl handed Dan a round pager.

"Thanks."

"I bet we wouldn't have a twenty-five minute wait at Wendy's," said Red, as he followed Dan through the crowd of people toward the bar.

"Yeah," Dan agreed, "but in here I can hardly hear you speak, so that's a plus."

"What?"

"Nothing."

Skip tapped Red on the shoulder. "Grab me a vodka martini, up, slightly dirty, with two olives," he said. "I've gotta drain the cobra."

"You got it," said Red.

"What can I get ya?" asked the bartender. He placed his palms on the edge of the bar and leaned forward to hear Dan better.

"Tequila, Seven, and lime," Dan said.

"Tequila Sunrise?" asked the bartender.

"Tequila. Seven. And lime," Dan repeated. He turned to Red. "What do you want?"

"LandShark draft."

"Where'd Skip go?"

"Toilet."

"What's he drinking?"

"Um … vodka something or other—just get him a beer too."

"And two LandSharks," Dan told the bartender.

A pager sitting on the bar vibrated and a man and woman got up from their bar stools. Dan and Red grabbed the seats.

The bartender placed their drinks in front of them and Dan paid.

"Hey," Red said.

"What?" Dan sipped his drink and then pulled the lemon wedge out of the glass and dropped it on the bar. "Moron," he mumbled. "Lime. Lemon. They don't even sound alike."

"You ever notice anything odd about Skip?"

"Everything I notice about him is odd," Dan replied.

"Yeah, but did you notice when he was talking to that Marilyn girl, he lost his surferesque style of talking. It's like it comes and goes. Whenever things get serious, he acts almost like a different person."

Dan nodded. "Yeah, I've noticed. It's happened a few times in the past."

"And he works part-time at a gas station but can afford his own house in Key West. He can't make much more than minimum wage. You think we should ask him about it?"

"If there was anything he wanted us to know, he would talk to us. Some people live in the Keys because they don't want to tell their story. Maybe he's one of them."

"I Googled him once."

"I hope you used protection."

"Funny."

"And what came up when you Googled him?"

"Nothing, really. I mean there's a lot of people with the name Sean Stoner, but none of them are him. You know, he has no Facebook account, or Instagram, or anything else like that."

"I don't either," Dan reminded his friend.

"Yeah, but Skip's younger than us. Most people his age spend half their day posting pictures on that shit."

"Maybe he's smarter than most of them."

"What's up, bromigos?" Skip shouted over the crowd. "That thing didn't buzz yet? What has two thumbs and needs to strap on the old feedbag? This dude!" He pointed at himself with his thumbs and then rubbed his almost non-existent belly. "Where's my martini?"

Red had an aha moment. "A martini!" He picked the pint glass up off the bar. "Here's your beer, pal."

"Thanks," Skip said disappointedly.

"Sorry."

"Don't worry about it, Red Man."

Just then the pager buzzed. They brought it back to the podium, and were shown to their seats. The three men scanned the menu, and when the waitress arrived, they placed their order.

Red nodded across the table to Dan. "Hey Skip," he said. "Where did you say you were from?"

Skip wasn't paying attention. He was more focused on a young blonde with mile-long legs sitting alone at the bar. Dan thought she looked like Heather Thomas. When he was a horny teenager Dan had a poster of the Fall Guy bombshell, wearing a skimpy pink bikini that left nothing to the imagination, on his bedroom wall. Back in the day, popping three balloons with three darts at a county fair could provide a thousand sexual fantasies for a young man.

"Skip!" said Red.

"What?" Skip answered annoyed.

"Where did you say you were from?"

Dan sipped his tequila.

"Why do you ask, Red Man?"

"Dan and I was just wonder—"

"I wasn't wondering anything," said Dan.

Skip didn't take his eyes off the young blonde across the room, who now aimed her megawatt smile at him. "We lived in Key West when I was a kid, and then we moved to San Diego when I was a teenager."

"Your dad was in the military?" Red asked.

"Sure was."

"Retired?"

"Retired from the military," Skip answered. "But he still works."

"What's he do?"

"He's with the FDLE in Jacksonville."

Dan caught Red's puzzled look. "Florida Department of Law Enforcement," he explained. "So, he's a cop?"

"Crime scene dude, to be specific," Skip clarified.

"Crime scene *dude*?" Red questioned.

"Let me out of the booth, Red Man," Skip said, scooting his butt closer to Red.

Red got up, and Skip excused himself from the table. Red sat back down. He and Dan watched him cross the room to the bar. He introduced himself to the young blonde and took a seat on the stool next to her.

"Remember when it was that easy?" Red commented.

"Not really," Dan replied.

Red turned back to Dan. "His father's a cop. Did you know that?"

"Nope."

When the waitress brought the plates to the table, Dan raised his hand to get Skip's attention. Skip looked over and grinned big. He gave Dan the thumbs-up.

Dan and Red were half-way through their meals when Skip finally returned to the table.

"Hey, I hate to ditch you guys," Skip said, "but I'm gonna take off."

"Take off?" Red asked. "What about your food?"

"Have her wrap it up and bring it back to the hotel for me. Thanks." Skip turned and hurried back to the bar.

"I can't believe he's taking off on us like that," Red complained.

"Are ya shittin' me?" Dan asked. "I'd take off too. Did you see how cute she was?"

"What about bros before hoes?"

"That's not a real thing," said Dan. "It's always hoes before bros, especially ones that look like Heather Thomas."

"Looks like Heather *Locklear* to me," Red remarked.

"You have your fantasies, I'll have mine.

On his way out the door Skip looked back at his two friends with a huge grin. He pointed down at the girl's butt and then gave another thumbs-up.

Dan and Red ordered another drink and finished their meals while trying to talk over the ear-splitting music of Luke Bryan and Florida Georgia Line. When the check came Red stared at his friend, waiting for him to pick it up.

"I suppose I'm paying," said Dan.

"If you insist," Red replied.

Dan left the money on the table, and the two men walked back across the highway toward the hotel. When Red arrived at his door he noticed the board shorts Skip had been wearing were now wrapped and tied around the doorknob.

"What the hell is this?" asked Red.

"I think that's the international surfer dude sign for 'if this room's ah rockin' don't come ah knockin.'"

"That's just great. Where am I supposed to sleep?"

"I guess you're in my room," Dan said, unlocking his door.

"You only have one bed."

"I did just buy you dinner," Dan joked.

"It would take more than dinner," Red shot back.

Dan cocked his head. "But I did get you to the bargaining table."

"Oh, shut up." Red followed his pal into the room. "You don't snore, do ya?"

"I don't know. I'm always asleep. But I do sleep naked."

"Not tonight ya don't."

Dan grabbed the remote and turned on the TV. "You're the most homophobic man I've ever met."

"Oh, sor-*ee* if sleeping with a naked man makes me homophobic."

Dan hopped on the bed and sat with his back against the headboard. He stretched his legs out in front of him and crossed them at the ankles. He smiled at Red and patted the spot next to him. "Come on, princess," he said.

"There is something seriously wrong with you," Red said, and went into the bathroom and shut the door.

Chapter Seventeen

At four in the morning Dan was awakened by the flashing of blue and red lights on the walls and ceilings of his room. At first he thought it was some weird dream about a discotheque. He rubbed his eyes and lifted his head.

"Hey," said Dan. He nudged Red's shoulder. "Hey!"

"Knock it off," Red replied.

"Hey!" Dan said, nudging him again.

"What?" Red rubbed the sleep out of his eyes and noticed the lights too. "Hey, what's all the commotion?"

Dan had gotten out of bed and on his way to the window. "I don't know." He parted the vertical blinds with the tip of his finger. "There's about half a dozen cop cars out there. They got that Steve kid next door in handcuffs."

Red swung his legs over the bed and started for the door. He had slept in his shorts and T-shirt. To Red's delight, Dan had also wore a T-shirt and boxers to bed.

Red opened the door and looked out. He stepped out onto the front walkway and Dan followed.

"Knock on Skip's door," Dan said.

A cop placed Steve Foster into the backseat of one of the squad cars. Steve turned his head and looked at Dan. The kid was scared. The officer shut the door, and Steve continued to stare through the window at Dan and Red.

Dan stepped off the sidewalk and onto the blacktop. He walked to the nearest officer. "What's going on?" he asked.

The officer pointed at Steve. "Kid abducted his ex-girlfriend yesterday and shot her mother."

"Marilyn Martin?" Dan asked.

"Who?"

"The girl, Marilyn Martin. We spoke to her and the Foster kid earlier this evening."

The cop shook his head. "No," he said. "The girl's name is Harrison … Maggie Harrison. Father's some big shot lawyer down in West Palm Beach."

Skip and Red walked up beside Dan.

"What's goin' on, Dan the Man?" Skip asked.

"That kid, Steve, he kidnapped that girl."

"Marilyn?" Skip asked.

"Yeah, but her name's not Marilyn," said Dan. "It's Maggie Harrison. He shot her mother too."

"Whoa, dude, that's bogus. I really believed that dude's story."

"Me too," said Dan.

"Is the mother okay?" Red asked.

"The mother's dead," said the cop.

They watched as the patrol car containing Steve Foster pulled out of the parking lot and disappeared from view.

"Where's the girl?" Dan asked.

"She's already on her way home," said the cop.

"Thanks," Dan said. He turned and walked back to his room with Red and Skip following behind him.

"I'm starving," Red commented.

"Me too," said Skip. "I burned off a lot of calories last night, if you know what I mean." He jabbed Red in the ribs with his elbow.

"Yeah, Skip, I know what you mean. Your dinner from last night is in the mini-fridge."

"Dude, there's no way those nachos survived the night. I'm gonna need to scarf down some eggs and bacon."

"Okay," said Dan, "we'll grab something on our way out of town."

Red and Skip walked into their room, and Dan went back to his. Dan walked to the nightstand and grabbed his cell phone. He opened his call log and dialed Maggie Harrison's number.

We're sorry, you have reached a number that has been disconnected or is no longer in service. If you feel you have reached this recording in error, please check the number and try your call again.

Dan hung up his cell phone. He knew there was no reason to try again. He himself had made the call with Maggie's phone, and knew he had dialed correctly. He put the phone back on the night stand, and went in to take a shower.

Chapter Eighteen

By seven o'clock the three amigos had eaten breakfast at IHOP and were on the Florida Turnpike headed toward Bonifay. Dan sat in the passenger seat staring at the screen of his cell phone.

"We're still five hours away," Dan commented.

"I didn't think it was supposed to take this long," said Red.

"It wouldn't have," Dan responded, "if shit stick hadn't of taken Route 27."

"It was supposed to be a shortcut," Skip shot back.

Dan put the cell back in his pocket. "We're not gonna be there till after noon."

"I wonder if they have any good lunch places there?" Red said.

"What the Christ?" said Dan, "You just ate a huge breakfast. 'All you can eat pancakes' is just a slogan. You didn't have to try and eat *all* of the pancakes."

Skip threw a thumb in Dan's direction. "Sounds like someone's a little jealous that the cooks didn't come out and applaud for *him*."

"I couldn't believe they gave me a T-shirt," said Red. "I didn't know they did that."

*****

At quarter to twelve Skip got off I-10 at exit 112 for Bonifay, Florida. At the end of the ramp he took a right onto South Waukesha Street.

"Wow," Red commented in amazement, "it's like restaurant row here. Waffle House, Burger King, Pizza Hut, Hardee's, McDonald's—ooh, a Mexican place!"

"I'm not riding in a car with you after you eat Mexican food," said Dan.

"It's a convertible," Red replied.

"Yeah, my past experiences with you tell me that wouldn't matter."

Red chuckled.

"Where to, Dan the Man?" Skip asked.

"Hardee's," Red answered.

"We'll eat after we talk to this guy," said Dan.

Red sat back in the seat and sighed loudly. "Whatever."

Dan stared at his cell phone. "Take a left up here on Brock Avenue."

Skip took the left, and then the next right onto McGee Road.

"North-west Florida looks nothing like southern Florida," Dan commented, as he looked around at the pine, cedar, and elm trees that lined the narrow streets. "I feel more like I'm back home in upstate New York." There was a tinge of nostalgia in his voice.

"Bonifay Nursing and Rehabilitation Center," said Red, reading a roadside sign aloud.

"It's right up here on the left," said Dan. He pointed at a white ranch-style home with black shutters that sat on the corner. "Right there."

There were no sidewalks or curbs on McGee Street so Skip pulled his Volkswagen into the other lane and parked off the road, partially on the grass, facing in the wrong direction. He shut off the engine. "What's the plan?" he asked.

"There's no plan," Dan replied. He reached into one of the pockets in his cargo shorts and pulled out a small stack of business cards held together with a pink rubber band. He pulled one of the cards from the stack and placed it into his front pocket with his money clip. He put the rest of the stack back where he got it and climbed out of the car. Skip and Red started to get out of the car as well.

"You guys wait here and let me talk to him by myself," said Dan. "We don't want to spook him."

Skip pulled his door closed. "You got it, Dan the Man."

On the right-hand side of the house was a dirt driveway. Seeing no sidewalk or pathway, Dan cut across the yard toward the front door. Corky Maddigan's lawn reminded Dan of his own lawn: more weeds and bare patches than grass, and about a dozen rusty-brown circles where neighborhood dogs had obviously taken a piss. Of course, in Dan's case, Buddy was the only culprit.

Dan knocked on the door and waited. After knocking a third time with no response, he walked to the far side of the house and looked up the driveway. Parked there, facing the street, was a blue 2012 Honda Civic. Dan's noted the absence of a front license plate. He knew it was probably somewhere on a green BMW. He went around to the back of the car. There was no rear plate either. Dan went around to the back door and knocked. He slowly turned in a circle and scanned the surrounding property. When he was facing the door again, he knocked once more.

The backdoor opened. "Hey, dude," said Skip, pulling the door all the way open. He had a funny look on his face. "Pretty ripe in here."

"What the Christ are ya doing in there?" Dan asked.

"The front door was unlocked," Skip replied.

"Where's Red?" Dan asked.

"In the living room looking at the dead guy. Follow me … or just follow your nose."

Red was in the living room, on his knees, next to the body of a forty-something male. The deceased was lying on his back, dressed in blue jeans and a white T-shirt. He was barefoot; the bottoms of his feet were filthy and calloused.

"Looks like he took three right through the chest," said Red.

Dan's eyes went from the small holes in the dead guy's chest to the dried blood stain beneath him on the carpet.

"Hmm. Judging by the body stiffness and skin lividity, rigor mortis and liver mortis are both well established," Skip observed. "Been dead a few days, I'd say. Since Tuesday, probably." Dan and Red exchanged an incredulous look. Skip quickly added, "Probably why he never reported his license plates being stolen."

"He got any ID?" Dan asked.

"I don't know," Red replied.

"Check his back pocket."

Red stood up and backed away from the body. "*You* check his back pocket."

Dan looked at Skip.

"I'll do it," Skip said. He knelt down, rolled the stiff onto his side, and shoved his fingers into the guy's back pocket. He pulled out a wallet and let the man fall back into place. He opened the wallet and pulled the man's driver's license from one of the slots. "Corky Maddigan." He put the ID back and handed the wallet to Dan.

"I guess this is what you would call a dead end," said Red.

Skip snickered. "Good one, Red Man."

Dan's cell phone rang. "Hey, Maxine."

"Hey yourself. Sorry I missed your call last night."

"Yeah, I figured you wouldn't call back until today. How's things going?"

"What's that?" Maxine asked. "You're cutting in and out."

"I asked you how things were going."

"Good. What's go —— *[crackle]* on *[crackle]* —— you?"

"What?"

"Good. What's going on with you?" Maxine repeated.

Dan looked down at the dead body. "Nothing, really. Pretty dead around here." He looked to Skip.

Skip pointed at Dan and snickered. "Good one, Dan the Man," he whispered.

"We're gonna grab some lunch in a bit and then probably question a few people. Hope to head back tonight."

"Hope to?"

"We'll see."

"Oh, Chief Carver stopped by this morning. He was looking for you."

"What did he want?"

"He said *[crackle]* —— still haven't *[crackle]* —— victim next door."

"What?"

"They still haven't ID'd the guy next door!"

"Did he ask where I was?"

"Yes. I told him you, Red, and Skip went fishing upstate."

"Good. What do you have planned for the day?"

"Stacy's art showing."

"Oh yeah. Sorry I'm missing that."

"I bet. Love ya."

"Back at ya." Dan hung up and put his cell back in his pocket. "Wow, bad service here."

"What now?" Red asked.

"Carver said they still don't have an ID on the dead guy we found in the Stewart's house."

"So, he's never been arrested before," said Skip.

Dan put Corky's wallet into his pocket and turned toward the front door. "Come on. Let's get out of here before someone sees us."

The three men headed toward Skip's waiting Thing.

"Lunch?" Red asked

"Yeah, sure," Dan replied. "After smelling Corky's rotting corpse for the last fifteen minutes, all I can think about is getting something to eat."

Chapter Nineteen

Red chose Hardee's for lunch and ordered the 2/3 pound Monster Thickburger with four strips of bacon, three slices of cheese, and extra mayonnaise. Skip got a taco salad and Dan ordered 1/4 pound cheeseburger.

"Oh, man, this is so good," Red said, after washing his second bite down with root beer.

"I can almost hear your heart trying to pump the lard through your veins," Dan said.

"I wish I could hear you shut up," Red shot back.

"You couldn't hear him if he shut—"

"I know, Skip," said Red.

Skip looked across the table at Dan. "What's our next move, dude?" he asked.

"We need to go back to Corky's house," Dan said.

"Why?" Red asked.

"Because our fingerprints are all over the doorknobs."

"You should have thought of that when we were there," Red groused around another mouthful.

"I was too busy trying not to vomit."

Skip made a squeamish face. "Same here, dude," said Skip. "Of course, I wrapped my shirt around the doorknobs when I opened them."

"Good thinking," said Dan.

"What if someone sees us?" asked Red.

"You and I will go door to door and ask questions while Skip sneaks in through the back door and wipes the place down. We'll wipe down the front doorknob when we knock on Corky's door. Hopefully by the time someone finds Corky's body, this will all be solved."

"You know, I've been thinking," Red remarked. "We shouldn't just leave him in there like that."

"What are we supposed to do with him?" asked Dan.

"We should call somebody."

"Who?"

"The cops."

"Then Rick will find out we were here."

"He's gonna find out eventually anyway."

"Yeah, but I'm hoping that will be after we solve this case."

"Carver is gonna be so pissed," said Skip.

"He's been pissed before, and this probably won't be the last time."

"He has been in a better mood lately," Red pointed out.

"This will probably end that," said Skip.

After lunch, the three men piled into Skip's Thing and drove back over to McGee Street. Skip parked the car in the same spot he had parked it earlier.

Corky Maddigan's house sat at the corner of McGee Street and McKinley Drive. McKinley Drive was in the shape of a horseshoe. If you entered McKinley near Corky's place and followed it around, you would eventually exit back onto McGee Street, about two hundred yards down the street from Corky's. The homes in Corky's neighborhood were sparse. He only had about nine neighbors, seven of those being on McKinley.

Dan pointed at the house to the north of Corky's. "Red and I will start at that house," he said. "Skip, you go back inside Corky's and wipe down the doorknobs and anything else we might have touched."

"Roger that, Dan the Man," Skip replied. He jumped up on his seat and leapt over the door. "Rally back here in say"—he glanced down at his wrist watch—"thirty minutes?"

"I probably won't 'rally' anywhere," Dan replied as he climbed out of the front passenger side seat. "We'll just start going door to door on McKinley Drive after we're finished at the first place."

Red chuckled. "You'll have to 'rally' with yourself, Skip."

"I think he 'rallies' himself a little too much," said Dan.

"Dudes, really?"

"Just bustin'," Dan assured him.

"So then what do you want me to do after I wipe the place down?"

"Just hang out. We shouldn't be long."

"Roger that," Skip said, and he headed for Corky's.

Dan and Red walked down the street about fifty yards to Corky's closest neighbor. The house looked a lot like Corky's house. It was a white ranch with black shutters. There was also a dirt driveway with no sidewalk leading to the front door. The biggest difference was that this house had a small concrete front porch with a shed roof over it and a for sale sign in the front yard.

Dan knocked on the door a few times and waited.

"Quiet neighborhood," Red commented. "Not one car has driven down this street other than us both times we were here."

"Yeah," Dan agreed. "As quiet as a graveyard."

"Good one, Dan the man."

Dan winced. "Cut it out. It's bad enough when Skip does it."

Dan knocked again.

As the door opened, Dan reached into his pocket for the business card.

"Yes?" asked the tall thin black man wearing sunglasses.

Dan held up the business card. "Good afternoon, sir," he said. "I'm Dan Coast, and his is my associate, Red Baxter."

The man stared at Dan. "You from the bank?" he asked.

Dan tried to hand the card to the man, but he wouldn't take it.

"No, sir. We were retained by the family of Corky Maddigan," Dan explained. "He's been missing for a few days and we were wondering if you might remember the last time you saw him."

"I don't remember the exact date," the septuagenarian answered. "But it was at least seven years ago." The man leaned slightly on the cane in his right hand.

"Seven years ago?" Red asked.

"You haven't seen Mr. Maddigan in seven years?" Dan asked. "Were the two of you in some sort of a dispute?"

"No, we get along great. He mows my lawn every week. We just had a beer together last Saturday after he mowed my lawn as a matter of fact."

Dan and Red looked at each other, then back at the man. "I thought you said you hadn't seen him in seven years?" said Dan.

"I haven't."

"I don't understand."

"I'm blind, ya fuckin' idiot! You think I wear these glasses fer a fashion statement?" The man pulled off the glasses to reveal his dead gray eyes. "I wear 'em so's people don't have to look at these."

"Oh," said Red disgustedly. "Put them back on, please."

"Sorry, sir," Dan said. He half-turned his head away from the old man's eyes. He felt a little Hardee's move into the back of his throat.

The guy slid the sunglasses back on. "Like I says, I had a beer with Corky on Saturday, and that's the last I heard ah him."

"He was reported missing on Tuesday," said Dan, doing his best to come up with a believable timeline. "Do you remember hearing anything odd next door, either that day, or maybe the day before?"

"Not that I recall."

"Did Corky seem any different than usual leading up to Tuesday?" Red asked.

"Not that I recall."

"Well, here's my card," Dan said.

"Is it in Braille?" asked the man.

"Well, no," Dan replied.

"Then what the hell am I gonna do with it?"

"Um," said Dan, "how about if you give me your number, and then I can give you a call when Corky is located."

"Shore," said the old man, and he rattled off his phone number.

Dan thanked him, and they left.

"You see those eyes?" Red whispered as they cut across the yard. "Holy shit! They looked like gray Jell-O with a green olive in the middle."

"Yeah," Dan said. "Let's never talk about those eyes again."

"It's a deal," Red agreed. "McKinley Drive?"

"Yut."

The first house Dan and Red came to was a salmon-colored single-story cinder block house that sat directly behind Corky's place. Unlike the houses on McGee, this one had a concrete driveway and a concrete path leading to the front door. No one was home at that house, or the one across the street from it.

After knocking on the third door, and having no luck, Red said, "You would think a few of these people would be home on a Saturday afternoon."

"Yeah," was Dan's reply.

Finally, as they approached the second curve in the street, a man in his early forties was riding his lawnmower around the front yard of his red-brick home. Dan gave the man a wave, and the man waved back. Dan and Red stopped at the edge of the man's property and waited. The man looked over at them again, and knowing they wanted to speak with him, he steered the mower toward them. He shut off the engine when he reached them.

"Good afternoon," Dan said. "I'm Dan Coast, and this is my associate, Red Baxter."

The man reached out his hand and they all shook. "Pete Maddigan," the guy said.

Dan and Red exchanged quick glances. Dan threw a thumb over his shoulder. "Are you related to Corky Maddigan?" he asked.

Pete rolled his eyes. "What did he do this time?"

"He hasn't done anything," said Dan. "We wanted to question him in connection with a motor vehicle accident."

"Are you cops?" asked Pete.

"No," said Dan. "We're working with the other party's insurance company."

"Where did this accident take place?" asked Pete.

"Key West."

"I didn't know my cousin had been to Key West recently."

"We don't think he had," Dan explained. "The vehicle that caused the accident had stolen license plates that traced back to Corky's vehicle. We were just at his residence and the plates are missing off his Honda Civic."

"I see. Have you been able to speak with Corky?"

"No. He wasn't home."

"Would you like me to give him a call?"

"That would be very helpful," said Red.

Dan and Red waited patiently as Pete called Corky on his cell phone. They exchanged glances knowing full well that Corky would not be answering that call, unless he had taken his cell phone with him into the great beyond.

"He's not answering," said Pete, hanging up and slipping the cell back into his front pocket.

"Darn it," said Red. "We were really hoping to speak with him."

"Do you know where he might be?" asked Dan. "Is there anyone he hangs out with a lot—a girlfriend, maybe?"

"He's probably with that pig, Sandy," Pete answered, shaking his head. "She's this married woman he's—"

"Dan the Man!" Skip shouted. "Dan!"

The three men turned to see Skip running down the road waving something in his hand. When he got to Dan he handed him a photograph.

Pete looked Skip up and down. "You're an insurance investigator too?" he asked suspiciously.

"He's my son," Red said. "He just wanted to come along for the ride today. Red smacked Skip in the back of the head. "Don't be runnin' off like that, boy."

Skip shot him a look. "Sorry, D*ad*," he said.

Dan looked at the photograph of Corky Maddigan with his arm around the woman who had hollered at Dan about dog shit and cigars almost a week earlier. The two were smiling big and leaning against a green BMW. The rear of Corky's house was in the background. Dan held up the photograph for Pete to see. "This Sandy?" he asked.

"Yeah, that's her," Pete answered. "Where ... did you get that picture?"

"It was taped to the inside door of Mr. Maddigan's shed," Skip replied.

"You know who might have taken this photograph?" Dan asked.

"Could have been Sandy's husband, Forrest," said Pete. "He and Sandy were always over to Corky's."

"Last name?" Dan asked.

"Franken ... or Franklin, maybe," Pete answered.

"Sandy's husband and Corky were friends?" Red asked.

"Not really," Pete replied. "I got the idea that it was Corky and Sandy who were friends, maybe even a little more than friends."

"That didn't bother Sandy's husband?" asked Dan.

"It didn't seem to, but who knows? I was only around them a few times. Seemed to me like they just used him.

He'd do odd jobs for them at their place. I don't even know if they paid him."

"You wouldn't have an address for Sandy and Forrest, would you?" Dan asked.

"I think they live somewhere outside of town, but I don't know where exactly."

"Do you remember the last time you saw Corky?" Red asked.

Pete looked to the clouds in thought. "Hmm. Last Thursday or Friday maybe. I can't be sure."

"Where did Corky work?" asked Red.

"Did?" asked Pete.

"Does," said Dan.

"Corky doesn't work. He's on permanent disability."

"What's his disability?" Dan asked.

Pete tapped the side of his head with his index finger. "Corky's a little funny."

"Funny?" asked Red. "Funny how?"

"He ain't the sharpest tool in the shed, if ya know what I mean. Fell out of a neighbor's tree when we were kids. Smacked his head against a cement block. He can drive, and take care of himself, but he can't hold down a job. Always had some anger issues. His parents left him the house. Nope, that man never worked for anything a day in his life. Shit just falls in Corky's lap. Oh, he mows his neighbor's lawn once a week, but that's about it."

"You know where Corky met Sandy?" Dan asked.

Pete cocked his head. "No," he replied. "What insurance company did you say you were with?"

"State Farm," Red replied, and at the same time Dan said, "Nationwide."

"Can I see that business card again?" Pete asked.

Dan patted his pockets. "Are you sure I didn't give it to you?"

"I'm sure."

"I coulda' swore I—"

"Do you only have one business card?"

"The rest are in the car. I think we have everything we need here. Thanks for your help Mr. Maddigan."

Pete didn't answer. He sat on his mower and watched as the three men rounded the corner. When they were out of sight, he reached down and restarted the engine, scratched his head, and returned to his mowing.

"Where did you really get that picture?" Dan asked.

"Corky's dresser drawer," Skip answered. "I looked the place over pretty good. I didn't see anything else. The dude's not much of a pack rat. Matter of fact, he doesn't have much of anything. Socks and underwear in some drawers and a few shirts and pants in the closet. The only photograph I found in the whole house was the one I gave you. There's no knickknacks on shelves, no photo albums. No keepsakes or souvenirs, no trophies. It's like he's never kept anything from his past."

As they walked back to the car, Dan thought about his own house. He didn't have anything from his past either. He was surprised that Skip had never noticed. Until Maxine moved in, he didn't even have pictures on the wall, or a couch for that matter. When Dan moved to Key West, he left his past behind, bringing only his dog and a small U-Haul trailer containing a couple boxes of clothing and a few pieces of furniture. Most of Dan's past was stored in his parents' garage, and a storage unit in upstate New York.

No one spoke the rest of the walk back to the car, which led Dan to believe that maybe Skip did remember that Dan's house was bare memories, just like Corky Maddigan's. Maybe Skip felt as though he had put his foot in his mouth and then decided to keep quiet for a while. It angered Dan that after almost five years, he still couldn't make it through an entire day without thinking about his deceased wife, Alex.

Once they were back in the Thing, Red noticed Dan's pensive mood. "Penny for your thoughts, pal," he said.

Dan glared at him. Red knew that look, and what it meant. He was thinking about his dead wife. Red gave Dan's shoulder a brotherly squeeze and held his tongue.

Chapter Twenty

Skip drove his Thing north two blocks and hung a right onto US-90. "I gotta get this old girl some petrol," he said. "I wonder where this town hides their gas stations."

Red pointed up the street. "There's an Exxon," he said.

Skip pulled off the road and up to the row of pumps, and shut off the engine.

Dan got out first. "I'll go in and pay," he said. "Anybody want anything?"

"I'll take a grape soda," Red called out. "And a bag of Cool Ranch Doritos."

Dan went inside and walked up to the register. He pulled out his money clip and tossed a fifty-dollar bill onto the counter. "How's it goin'?" he asked the guy behind the counter. The patch on his shirt said Merle.

"Can't complain," the guy responded. "Even if I did—"

"No one would give a shit," Dan said, finishing Merle's sentence.

Merle chuckled. He picked up a Mountain Dew bottle off the counter that he had been using as a spitter all day, and brought it up to his lips. He spit a good amount of Skoal juice into it and put it back down. He wiped his chin with the back of his hand. "Ain't that the truth," he said. "Just the gas?"

Dan remembered Red's order and spun around. "Nope. I need some Doritos and a grape soda."

Dan walked down the chip aisle and searched, but there were no Cool Ranch, so he settled on Nacho Cheese. He grabbed a Crush Grape Soda out of the cooler and returned to the counter. "I guess this'll do it, Merle."

Merle rang up his order. "That'll be $46.11 with the gas."

Dan slid the fifty to Merle, and Merle made change. "There you go. You have a nice day, ya here?"

"Thanks, Merle," Dan replied. "You too."

Merle looked down at his name patch. "It's Darwin," he said.

"What's that?"

"Name's Darwin. Spilt ketchup on my shirt earlier so I put Merle's shirt on."

"Gotcha," Dan said. "You have a nice day, Darwin."

Darwin nodded.

Dan turned back. "Oh, one more thing, Darwin." Dan reached into his pocket and pulled out the photograph. He held it up so Darwin could see it. "You know any of the people in this photo?"

Darwin leaned over the counter to get a better look. "Shore do," he replied, pointing his stubby finger at the picture. "That there's Corky. He lives over on McGee."

"Do you recognize the woman? Her name is Sandy … either Franklin or Franken. She has a husband named Forrest."

"No. Can't say I do. Just ol' Corky. Why you lookin' for Corky?"

"I'm not. It's the woman we're looking for. Corky just happens to be in the picture. Do you remember the last time you saw Corky?"

"Let me think. I would say … a little over a week ago."

"You ever see him driving the car in this picture?"

"The Beamer? No, Corky's got an old Honda Civic he drives around. He couldn't afford no Beamer. He don't work. He's a little wacky."

"Well thanks for your help, Merle."

"Darwin."

"That's right." Dan turned and left the building and walked back to Skip's car.

"What took ya so long in there, bro?" Skip asked. "I was just about to come in and check on ya."

Dan tossed the chips into the back seat.

"I said Cool Ranch," Red informed him.

"They didn't have any." Dan handed Red the soda. "I was just asking the guy in there if he knew the woman in the photograph." He opened the door and got in.

"And?" Skip asked. He turned the key in the ignition and the Thing sputtered and coughed to life

"He knew ol' Corky, but he never saw the woman before, or the green BMW."

Skip piloted the yellow metal box out of the Exxon. "Where to, navigator?" he asked Dan

"Turn here on Waukeshaw, and we'll see if we can get a room at the Holiday Inn."

"Were staying another night?" Red asked.

"Corky's cousin said that Sandy and her husband live somewhere around here" Dan responded. "We need to find that woman."

"Did I mention I have a business to run?" Red asked.

"Did I mention that everyone who works for you is better at running it than you are?" Dan shot back.

"You're an asshole."

"You're a—"

"Boys! Boys!" Skip hollered. "I'll turn this car around right now."

Chapter Twenty-One

After checking into the Bonifay Holiday Inn Express & Suites, Dan went to his room, and Red and Skip went next door to their room. Fifteen minutes later, the three men met down stairs in the dining area. Red and Skip sat at a round four-top near the television. Dan grabbed himself a cup of coffee from the complimentary coffee bar. Red was still eating his Doritos and drinking his grape soda.

"You want a coffee, Skip?" Dan asked.

"I'm good, bro," Skip replied.

Dan brought his paper to-go cup to the table and sat across from Red. He reached in the bag and pulled out a few Doritos, and stuffed them into his mouth.

"What's next?" Red asked.

"I'm gonna give Lou and Alice Stewart a call and see if they've ever heard of Sandy and Forrest Franklin or Franken."

"Good idea," said Skip.

Dan looked back over his shoulder at the young woman behind the registration desk. He pulled the photograph out of his pocket, got up, and walked over. "Excuse me," he said.

"Yes?" she asked. "Is everything okay?"

"Yes, everything is fine." Dan placed the picture on the desk. "Have you ever seen either of the people in this picture?"

The woman pushed her hipster glasses up her nose and bent down for a better look. "Why, yes," she said. "That's Corky Maddigan."

Everybody knows Corky, Dan mused. "How about the woman? Her name is Sandy ... Franken, or Franklin. She has a husband named Forrest."

She studied the photo. "Don't think I've ever seen her before."

"Do you recognize the car?"

"No, but I'm sure it's not Corky's. He has an old Honda he drives around. He lives over on McGee Street, a little ways past the nursing home."

Dan picked up the photograph. "Thank you."

"Is Corky in some kind of trouble?"

"No. It's not Corky we're looking for, it's the woman."

"Sorry I couldn't be more help," she said in a flirtatious voice that made it clear she wished Dan would ask her something else.

"I'm sorry for taking up your time."

Dan smiled at her. A million years ago a woman whose name he couldn't remember had said his smile was as sexy as Paul Newman's. He guessed it still was, because the clerk smiled back at him, and held his gaze for about a second too long. She wasn't half bad looking, if a little on the nerdy side. She reminded Dan of those prim women in old movies and TV shows who, when they took off their glasses and let their hair down, became instant sexpots. *Down, boy*, Dan warned himself. *Remember, you're an engaged person now.*

Dan walked back to the table and sat down.

"She recognize her?" Red asked.

"Nope, but she recognized ol' Corky. He's like a goddamn celebrity around here." Dan took out his cell and dialed.

"Hello?" said Rick Carver.

"Hey, Rick. It's Dan."

"Yeah, I know."

"Maxine said you called earlier."

"What?"

"Maxine said you called."

"Where —— *[crackle]* you?"

"Red, Skip, and I are fishing up at Lake Monroe. A buddy of Skip's has a camp up here."

"Must be nice."

"Maybe next time you can come."

"What's that?"

"Maybe you can come next time."

"Yeah, maybe."

"Maxine said you still didn't have an ID on the deceased."

"Nothing came —— *[crackle]* on *[crackle]* —— prints. We started circulating *crackle* — photograph this afternoon. Maybe *[crackle]* —— *[crackle]* —— kick back on that."

"What was the cause of death?" Dan asked.

"What?"

"Cause of death?"

"We must have a bad signal."

"Bad cell service up here. Cause of death?"

"The guy had a heart attack."

"So, no foul play?"

"No. Just a *[crackle]* —— old heart attack."

"I wonder why the woman took off then."

"All I can figure is that she wasn't supposed to be there with him. Maybe he's married and the woman was a girlfriend. Maybe she just got scared and took off."

"Yeah, maybe. I'm gonna let you go."

"What?"

Dan hung up his cell and placed it on the table. "The dead guy at the Stewart's place had a heart attack," he told Red and Skip.

"Then why did the woman take off?" Skip asked.

"Rick's theory is that the guy might have been having an affair and she was his girlfriend."

"Well, we know that probably ain't true," said Red.

"That's the only thing we know so far," said Skip.

"We know more than that," Dan argued. "We know Corky Maddigan is dead. We know Corky was friends with Sandy and Forrest Franken."

"Or Franklin," said Red.

"We're pretty sure the dead guy at the Stewarts' place is Forrest," Dan added.

"We are?" asked Red.

"I figured it was him," said Skip.

"Why would Sandy just leave her dead husband layin' on the floor like that and leave?" Red pondered.

"Maybe he died after she left," Dan offered.

"Maybe she didn't like her husband," Skip threw in. "Maybe she really liked Corky."

"Then who killed Corky?" Red asked.

"Maybe it was Forrest," Dan replied.

"Lot of maybes here," said Red. "I wonder how the blind neighbor figures into all this?"

Dan threw his friend a confused look. "Who the Christ said the blind guy had anything to do with this?"

"I don't know," said Red. "There's just something I don't trust about blind people."

Dan's expression went to complete surprise. "Wow! What? What the Christ don't you trust about blind people?"

"I don't know," Red admitted. "Just the way they can't see anything. It creeps me out."

"That doesn't make any sense at all."

"Maybe not to you, but to me it makes perfect sense."

"How do you feel about deaf people?" asked Skip.

"Don't even get me started," Red replied.

"Wow," Dan repeated. "I learn something new about you every day."

"I'm a man of many layers."

"A man of many layers that don't like blind and deaf people," Dan added.

"Now you're putting words in my mouth," Red shot back. "I never said I didn't like them. I said they just creeped me out a little bit. You know, the way some people are afraid of clowns."

"So it's that you're afraid of them?"

"Not exactly afraid of—you know what, let's just drop this."

"Gladly," said Dan.

"How do you feel about the song 'Pinball Wizard'?" asked Skip.

"How do *you* feel about shutting the hell up?" Red returned. "Forget I said anything."

"I'll never forget this conversation," Dan responded. "I'll probably bring this up once a week."

"So what else do we know?" Red asked, trying to change the subject.

"You mean besides knowing about your hatred for the physically impaired?" Dan asked.

"Oh my God!"

"Seriously," Skip said through his laughter. "We need to find out where these Franklin or Franken people live."

Red sat staring at his soda can and sulking as Dan went back to the registration desk to see if there was a phone book he could borrow. When he returned to the table, he tossed it in front of Red.

"See if they're in here," said Dan.

"Look for yourself," said Red.

"Okay, I will," said Dan. He sat back down in his chair and started flipping through the pages. When he got to the F's, he ran his finger down the page looking for Franken. "Dan pointed at an end table next to a sofa on the other side of the room. "Skip, grab that pen and letterhead."

Skip jumped up and went for the notepad as Dan continued his search.

When Skip returned to the table he readied himself to write.

"There's an F. Franken at 1846 North Waukesha Street. There's an S Franken at 2842 Linwood Circle. And there's a Sandra Franklin at 2097 State Route 17." When Dan reached the name Fynmore, he said, "I guess that's it," and closed the phone book.

Skip finished jotting down the names and addresses and pushed the notepad across the table to Dan. Dan read the names aloud.

"Start with Sandra Franklin?" Skip suggested.

"Good a place as any," said Dan. He glanced over at Red, who appeared to still be pissed from the ribbing he had gotten. Dan placed his hand on Red's forearm. "You hungry, princess?"

"Shut up."

"Are ya?"

"I could eat."

"There ya go," said Dan. "We was only bustin' your ovaries."

"You go too far sometimes."

"Where would you like to eat?"

"Cancun Mexican Grill."

"Okay, pal."

"Hey," said Skip, "I gotta sleep in the same room with him tonight."

"We all have our crosses to bear," said Dan. He picked up his cell phone again and dialed.

"Hello?"

"Alice?" Dan asked.

"Yeah. Who's this?"

"It's Dan Coast."

"Hey, Dan. Is everything okay?"

"Yeah, Alice. Everything is fine. You heard anything from Chief Carver?"

"He called yesterday to let us know that that poor man in our house died of natural causes."

"Okay. Did he also tell you they still don't know who he is?"

"Yes, he said that."

"Okay. I also had a question for you."

"What is it?"

"Do you know anyone by the name of Sandy or Forrest Franklin?"

"No. Should I?"

"Well, I'm up in Bonifay, Florida and—"

"What are you doing up there?"

"I traced the green BMW that was parked in your driveway back to here, so I came up to do a little investigating of my own."

"Chief Carver didn't mention that to me."

"He doesn't know I'm up here, Alice."

"What does the BMW have to do with those two people—Franklin, did you say?"

"Yes. Sandy and Forrest."

"You think that's who was at our house?"

"That's what we're thinking."

"We're?"

"Red Baxter is up here with me. We believe the dead man is Forrest Franklin. We came across a photograph of Sandy Franklin. She's the woman I saw at your house in the green BMW. There's another man in the picture with her named Corky Maddigan. Does that name ring a bell?"

"No. Who gave you all of these names?"

"Corky's cousin, Pete Maddigan. He lives around the corner from Corky."

"Did you speak with this Corky fellow?"

"Um … no. We, uh … knocked on his door but he didn't answer."

"I see. And what reason would these people have for being at our house?"

"That I don't know yet, but we'll keep digging. We're going to spend the night here in Bonifay at the Holiday Inn tonight, and snoop around some more tomorrow."

"Okay, Dan," said Alice. "Thanks for everything."

"Oh, and Alice—if you speak with Chief Carver again, don't mention to him that we're up here."

"I'll be sure not to."

Dan hung up the cell and put it in his pocket. "Shall we get something to eat?" he asked.

Red was on his feet in an instant. "Sounds good to me."

Dan folded the paper with the addresses and slipped it into his back pocket. On their way out the door, he dropped the phone book back at the front desk, and tossed his empty coffee cup into the trash bin.

The three men climbed into Skip's car and headed out of the parking lot. They drove between the Burger King and the People's South Bank that sat between their hotel and Waukesha Street. Skip turned right onto Waukesha, and drove down the street a little ways to the Cancun Mexican Grill.

Skip pulled into the parking lot and into the first spot he found. Saturday evenings were pretty busy at the Cancun Mexican Grill. As the three men crossed the blacktop toward the door, Dan paused and grabbed Red's arm.

"Hey, buddy," said Dan.

"What?" Red asked.

"You want me and Skip to go in first and check for hearing aids and white canes?"

"I hate you so much."

"I know you do, pal."

Chapter Twenty-Two

By the time Dan, Red, and Skip finished their meals, had a couple drinks, and returned to their hotel, it was a little after eight o'clock.

"I think I'm gonna hit the pool," said Red.

"If there's water in it, dude," Skip said.

"I already checked," Red responded. "There is."

"Whaddaya think, Dan the Man, should we take a dip as well?"

"I'll sit by the pool, but I'm not going in," Dan replied.

The three men entered the hotel and went straight for the elevator. Dan glanced over at the front desk to see that the younger woman from earlier in the day had now been replaced by a nice looking gray haired woman in her mid-sixties. Dan nodded and smiled.

"How y'all doin' this fine evening?" asked the woman. She smiled big.

"Wonderful," Dan returned.

Skip hit the up button on the elevator and they waited for the doors to part.

Once inside Red said, "I can't believe you're not going for a swim."

"I can't believe you have to go for a swim every time you're at a hotel," Dan replied.

"What's wrong with that?" Red said. "I like to use the menities."

"Oh do ya?" Dan asked. "It's *a*-menities, and I don't see you using the workout room."

"Amenities?" Red asked. "Are you sure?"

"Pretty sure."

The doors parted and the men stepped off the elevator.

"I'll meet ya down stairs in fifteen," said Red.

Dan turned to Skip in the hallway. "Is there still tequila in that bottle you brought?"

"Of course, bro. You want me to bring it down to the pool?"

"Yeah," Dan answered. "You bring the tequila and cups, I'll bring the ice and grab some 7UP out of the vending machine."

"It's a plan, Dan the Man."

Dan went into his room and Skip followed Red into theirs.

Dan walked to the edge of the bed, pulled out his cell, and dialed.

"Hello?"

"Hey, Maxine."

"How's the big case —— *[crackle]*?"

"We got some names, but that's about it. How was the art show?"

"It *[crackle]* —— really nice."

"Did you buy anything?"

"Uh … yeah."

"How much did you spend?"

"We'll *[crackle]* —— about it when *[crackle]* —— *[crackle]* —— home."

Dan was getting used to deciphering the staticky phone calls of late. "That don't sound good."

"When are you *[crackle]* —— to fix this window and ceiling?"

"I'll start on it as soon as I get home Tuesday."

"Tuesday? I thought you were going to be back tomorrow."

"Probably won't be back till really late Monday night. Do you mind?"

"No. would you mind if I just hired someone to fix this window? Rick said he has a guy—"

"No, Maxine."

"Why not? *[Crackle]* —— it'll get done."

"It'll get done when I do it."

"But I want it done some time this year. Pleeeeease."

Dan sighed loudly. He waited for Maxine to say never mind. She didn't. "Fine. Go ahead and call Rick's guy."

"Thank *[crackle]* ——."

"This guy better not be young and good-looking."

"He is. I already checked him out on Facebook."

"What the Christ?"

"I'm joking!"

"I gotta go."

"Love you."

"Back at ya." Dan hung up the cell and went into the bathroom.

*****

Skip and Red were already poolside when Dan arrived with the ice bucket, three bottles of 7UP, and the two bags of chips he had gotten from the vending machine. Skip had his cell phone on one of the plastic tables, next to his car keys; it was playing beach music. Skip sat shirtless and shoeless in one of the white plastic lounge chairs. Dan took a good look at him. The young man's grotesquely angular, pencil-thin body reminded Dan of Jeremy Duncan, the slacker main character in the comic strip *Zits*. Skip was tapping the armrest to the beat of the Beach Boys' "Little Deuce Coupe." Dan liked the Beach Boys, but he hoped this wasn't an entire playlist of surfer tunes.

He put the soda, ice, and chips on the table and took a seat on a lounge next to Skip.

Red walked around the pool stretching his arms over his head and slowly twisting and contorting his torso. He looked like Michael Phelps' out of shape, idiot cousin, preparing for a dog paddle race.

"Are you going in, or what?" Dan asked.

"I gotta test the water first," Red replied.

As he came around the pool, he stopped in front of Dan and Skip, and stuck in his big toe. "Yeah, I don't know, it's pretty cold. I might just—"

Dan jumped up and shoved him in.

Red shot back to the surface gasping for air. "You bastard!" he shouted.

Dan and Skip roared with laughter.

"I had to do it!" Dan shouted.

Red stayed in the pool and swam around while Skip made everyone a drink. He handed Dan his drink first.

"This is fun, Dan the Man," said Skip. "We should do stuff like this more often."

"Yeah," Dan agreed. "Let's make a pact. The next time one of us finds a dead body in the house next door to him, we'll all go on a road trip."

"It's a deal," Skip said.

Dan sipped his drink and watched his big friend do underwater somersaults.

"I take it we're gonna start checking those addresses first thing in the morning," Skip surmised.

"I think that should be the next step," Dan agreed.

Skip brought his glass to his lips; it exploded in his hands just as the two heard the gunshot.

Red was below the surface and heard nothing.

Skip rolled to his left off the lounge and onto the concrete. Dan did the same, rolling to his right.

Another shot rang out and one of the soda bottle ruptured, raining 7UP down upon them.

"Where's it coming from?" Skip shouted.

"Shit if I know,"Dan yelled. "Keep your head down!"

Just as Red surfaced a third shot sounded, a fourth. The end table exploded in a shower of plastic confetti. The tequila bottle shattered, producing a salvo of glass daggers.

Skip grabbed his car keys off the concrete and ran for the parking lot.

"Get down, you idiot!" Dan hollered, but Skip ignored him. Dan leapt to his feet to follow.

As Dan rounded the corner of the building another bullet hit the stucco, blasting shrapnel into the side of his face. He stutter-stepped and almost went down. When he reached the edge of the parking lot, Skip was pulling a pistol from the go-bag in his trunk.

Skip scanned the area, pointing the pistol in the direction of the gunfire.

They heard two car doors slam shut. "There!" Dan shouted, pointing at a dark sedan parked behind a dumpster situated between the hotel parking lot and the Burger King.

The headlights came on and the rear tires squealed.

Skip was now running at full speed through the Burger King parking lot in pursuit of the sedan. He made several attempt to aim his weapon as he ran, but there were too many cars and people. The sedan rounded the corner onto Waukesha Street, sending a hubcap rolling across the street and into a vacant lot. The vehicle fishtailed several times before the driver was able to regain control.

Skip ran into the center of Waukesha. As cars honked and whizzed around him in both directions, he took aim. He fired three times. The first two rounds hit the trunk and the third shattered the rear window. He dropped his weapon to his side and watched as the car drove out of sight.

Skip turned and walked back toward Dan, who was standing at the edge of the street. "Give me your shirt," said Skip bluntly.

Dan didn't ask why. He pulled his black T-shirt off and handed it to Skip. Skip's cheek and lip were bleeding, as well as the hand he'd been holding his glass with. There was a gash over his right eye. Skip rubbed his prints off the 9mm and wrapped it in Dan's T-shirt.

"What are ya gonna do with that?" Dan asked.

"Get rid of it," Skip replied.

"Probably a good idea."

The sirens were already wailing off in the distance.

Dan and Skip met Red in the hotel parking lot.

"What the hell was that?" Red asked.

Dan just shrugged his shoulders.

The three men returned to the pool.

"I'll be right back," Skip said. He jumped the fence and disappeared into the woods behind the hotel. He returned just as three police cruisers pulled into the parking lot.

"All taken care of?" Dan asked.

"You know it, bro," Skip responded.

Dan and Red gave each other a look. What's our story?" Red asked.

"Tell everything just like it happened, but eliminate the part about me having a gun and firing three rounds into the escape vehicle."

"But that was the cool part," Red argued.

"Thanks, Red Man," Skip said. "And those underwater somersaults you were doing were pretty radical as well."

Chapter Twenty-Three

Three hours later, light bars on what seemed like every cop car in the county were still flashing in the vicinity of the Bonifay Holiday Inn Express. Skip had a butterfly bandage on his right cheek, and another one over his right eye. The paramedics informed him that the wound would probably need stitches. He declined the offer for a ride to the nearest hospital.

Dan sat on the rear bumper of an ambulance that was parked in the parking lot, with his head tilted back, while a paramedic poured saline solution into his eyes.

"I think I got everything out of there," said the paramedic, "but your cornea is scratched up pretty good. It's gonna sting for a few days. Try not to rub it."

"Thanks," Dan replied, and rubbed his eye with his fingertips.

"Yeah, like that," said the paramedic.

"We have a witness that says he saw you with a gun," said a plain-clothes detective.

Skip snickered. "That dude must have been smokin' somethin' pretty good," he replied. "Guns are somethin' this hombre don't believe in. I'm a lover, not a fighter, bromigo."

The detective stared at Skip for a second. "Right," he responded, and looked to Red, who was standing next to Skip. "Do any of you carry a weapon?"

"No," said Red. "Like we've already told you, we were just sitting by the pool minding our own business when we heard the shots."

The detectives referred to his notes. "And you say the three of you are just up here on a road trip?"

"That's right, dude," Skip replied.

"When were you planning on leaving the area?"

"Tomorrow ... around lunch time," Red answered.

The detective closed his notepad.

"So, like, are we free to go back to our rooms?" Skip asked.

"Sure, *dude*," the detective mocked. "I have your contact information if I have any more questions." He turned and walked over to two uniformed officers who were standing nearby. The detective spoke with them. He looked back at Red and Skip a few times as he spoke.

"You think he believes us?" asked Red.

"Sure, dude," Skip replied. "Why wouldn't he? We're just three amigos on a road trip."

Dan walked up between the two men. He was still itching his eye.

"You probably shouldn't be rubbing that eye like that," Red informed him.

"Thanks, Dr. Baxter," Dan replied. "I'll take that under advisement."

"Who do you think it was?" asked Skip.

"My money is on Pete Maddigan," Dan replied.

"Corky's cousin?" Red asked. "Why would he try to kill us?"

"Maybe he found Corky's body and thinks we done it."

"Wouldn't he have just called the police?"

"Not if he's somehow connected to all this," said Skip.

"All what?" asked Red.

"Exactly," Dan responded.

"I'm confused," Red said.

"Me too," Dan admitted.

"What's next?" Red asked.

"I'm going to bed," Dan answered.

The three men walked across the parking lot and into the lobby of their hotel. Dan veered off toward the vending machine. "Anyone want a soda?" he asked.

"I'll pass," said Skip.

"No thanks," Red said, and walked onto the elevator.

Dan searched his pockets for change but found none. "Excuse me," he said to the woman at the desk.

She looked up from the newspaper she had spread in front of her and smiled. "Yes?"

"Can I get some change for the vending machine?"

"You sure can, hon."

Dan handed her a ten-dollar bill and she handed him back a five and five ones.

"Thanks," Dan said. "Is it always this exciting around here?" He reached into his pocket for the photograph of Corky and Sandy.

"Not hardly," said the woman. "There's been more excitement around here in the last week or so than there's been in the last forty years."

"What do you mean, last week or so?" Dan asked.

"Well, first the bank robbery, and now this."

"Bank robbery? When was that?"

"Hmm, let me see … Thursday before last." She continued to appear in deep thought for a second and then finally snapped out of it. "Yes, it was definitely last Thursday," she said, nodding her head.

"Did they catch who did it?" Dan asked.

"No, as a matter of fact, there hasn't been an arrest yet. The newspaper said there were very few clues left behind, and no one has offered any information." She turned her newspaper around and pushed it toward Dan. "It's all in here. There's even an interview with the bank president." The woman began folding the paper. "Here, you can take this. I'm all done with it."

"Thanks," Dan said, taking the paper in one hand, and laying the photograph on the desk with his other. "Do you know either of the two people in this photograph?"

She instantly pointed at Corky. "That's Corky Maddigan, he lives over on McGee Street." She picked up the picture and held it closer. "Don't know the woman."

"You ever see Corky driving this green BMW before."

She shook her head. "Nope."

"Thanks."

Dan turned and went to the vending machine. He got a bottle of ginger ale and a small bag of Famous Amos Chocolate Chip cookies.

Once in his room, he stripped down to his boxers and climbed on the bed. With the sound turned down on an old episode of The Twilight Zone, and a copy of the Times Advisor in his hands, he read all about the bank robbery that had occurred only nine days earlier.

According to the interview with Bonifay's police chief, the robbers got away with a little over eighty grand. The police had no suspects, and the scanty leads had turned up nothing. Dan found no obvious connections to the bank robbery and Corky Maddigan, or Sandy and her husband Forrest, but he couldn't shake the feeling that there was one. And why, if he was among the ambushers shooting at them earlier, did Pete Maddigan want them dead? Was he involved in the bank robbery, and wanted to permanently end their snooping?

Dan folded the paper and laid it on the nightstand next to the bed. He grabbed the remote control and turned the TV up just enough to hear it. The last episode of *The Twilight Zone* had ended, and a new one was starting. It was the episode titled "The Monsters Are Due on Maple Street," starring Claude Akins. It was one of Dan's favorite *Twilight Zone* episodes. He twisted the cap off the ginger ale and took a sip. He opened his package of cookies and tossed a couple into his mouth. He reached over and turned off the lamp and settled in to watch the show with great anticipation. He was asleep within fifteen minutes.

Chapter Twenty-Four

The Holiday Restaurant sat at the corner of Waukesha Street and US 90, right behind the Econo Lodge. The following morning, Dan, Red, and Skip sat at a four top in the restaurant studying their menus. Dan's copy of the *Times Advisor* lay folded on the table next to him.

"I'm gonna get pancakes," Red informed his cohorts.

"That sounds good," said Skip. He folded his menu and placed it at the corner of the table.

"Coffee?" asked the waitress when she arrived at their table.

"Yes, please," said Dan. He slid his cup closer to her.

She poured the three cups and said she would be back to take their orders in a second. All three men watched her strut away.

"Wow," Skip said."Bromigos, that's what I call poetry in motion."

"Yeah," Red agreed. "If I was ten years younger—"

"You'd still be a dirty old man," Dan finished for him. He picked up the newspaper, unfolded it, and dropped it in front of his cohorts.

"STILL NO SUSPECTS IN THE PEOPLES SOUTH BANK ROBBERY," Skip read aloud. "When did that happen?"

"Two Thursdays ago," Dan replied.

Red did the math in his head. "Ten days ago. Five days before you saw Sandy Franklin next door at the Stewarts."

"You think there's a connection?" asked Skip.

Dan shrugged. "I don't know. Maybe."

"You think her and her husband robbed the bank?" Red asked.

"Yeah, and what went on between Thursday and Tuesday?" asked Skip.

Dan shrugged again. "I said I don't know."

"Okay," asked the waitress, "what can I get for you gentlemen?"

They all ordered, and the young waitress wiggled away again. No one spoke until she was out of sight.

"You think Corky and his cousin Pete were in on it?" Skip asked.

"I bet the blind guy has something to do with it," Red offered.

"Yeah, I bet he did," Dan said, shaking his head. "I doubt he was the one taking shots at us last night, though."

"You never know," Red argued. "He missed every shot."

Skip laughed. "You got a point there, Red Man."

Dan removed the picture of Corky and Sandy from his pocket and placed it on top of the newspaper. He also pulled out the paper with the three addresses on it at and set it next to the photo. "After breakfast we'll check these places out and see if anything turns up."

"Anything like what?" Red asked.

"Anything like anything," Dan responded.

A different waitress stopped at the table with a coffee pot. "All y'all need a warm up?" she asked.

"Sure," Dan said. "Thanks."

She topped off each mug.

Dan pointed at the photograph. "You know either of these people in this picture?" Dan asked. "No, wait. Let me guess: you know that guy, right?"

The waitress gave him a quizzical look. "Well, sure. That there's Corky. He comes in here for breakfast and lunch all the time. Nice guy. A little odd. But ain't we all?" Her braying laugh ended in a piggish snort.

"Uh, yeah," said Dan. "The woman look familiar?"

"Can't say I ever seen her before. I'm new in town, so I don't know lots a folks yet. But workin' here, I'll get to know 'em all in no time."

"Do you remember the last time you saw Corky in here?"

"Let me think," she said, scratching her chin in thought. "He hasn't been in here this week that I know of. Middle of last week some time, I guess. Why y'all lookin' for him?"

"It's not him we're looking for," said Dan. "It's the woman."

The waitress turned and saw Dan's waitress at another table. "Maggie!" she called out.

Maggie turned. "Yeah, Phyllis?"

"Come here for a second."

Maggie finished up at the other table and walked over.

"You know this woman?" asked her coworker.

Dan took a big gulp of his coffee.

"Sandy?" Maggie asked. "Yeah, I know her. Her and her husband, Forrest, live out at the old Stewart place on State Route 173."

Dan did a spit take. "What?" he spluttered. He coughed a few more times and reached for his napkin. "Stewart place?" He wiped his chin.

"Yeah," said Maggie. "Mr. and Mrs. Stewart's farm— well, it's not a farm any more. Mr. Stewart passed away about five years ago, and his wife soon after. Their son, Lou, has the place now … him and his wife, Alice."

"Where do the Franklin's fit in?" Red asked.

"They rent the old farm house from the Stewart's," Maggie replied.

"Well isn't that something," said Skip.

"Thanks for your help, Maggie," Dan said.

"Sure thing."

Maggie and Phyllis left the table. "Well how do you like that?" Dan remarked. "Alice said she had never heard of Sandy and Forrest Franklin."

"And at least we know for sure that it *is* Franklin and not Franken," Red threw in.

"Yeah, because that matters," Dan responded.

"You gonna give the Stewarts a call back?" Skip asked.

"I think we'll head out to the *old Stewart farm* first," Dan replied, "and see what Sandy Franklin is up to."

"The Stewarts must be involved in this whole thing," said Skip, "or Alice wouldn't have lied."

"I can't imagine that Alice and Lou are bank robbers," Dan said.

"Should we go back and speak to the blind guy?" Red asked.

"Drop it with the blind guy!"

Chapter Twenty-Five

Skip slowed the Volkswagen Thing to about forty-five miles per hour as he approached the Stewart farm.

"Son of a bitch," Dan said, when he immediately recognized Lou Stewart's brand new Buick Regal. The sport red four-door sat parked near an out building between the house and the barn.

"You think Sandy Franklin is holding the Stewart's against their will?" Red asked.

"We'll soon find out," Dan said

"Should I pull in?" Skip asked.

"No, keep driving," Dan replied.

"I get it," said Red. "Sneak up on them after dark. Good idea."

"No, we'll sneak up on them as soon as we find a good place to hide the car," said Dan.

Skip reached under the seat and pulled out the 9mm that was still wrapped in Dan's bloody T-shirt. He handed the weapon to Dan.

"When did you grab this?" Dan asked.

"Early this morning," Skip replied. "You didn't think I would leave it in the woods like that, did ya, bro?"

"I never know what to think with you, Skip."

"I'll take that as a compliment, my friend."

Dan unwrapped the weapon and placed it on the seat next to him. He held up his bloody shirt. "I loved this shirt," he said wistfully.

"It's just a T-shirt," said Red.

"But it was one of my favorites."

"Okay, so we'll give it a proper burial later," Red promised.

"Not likely," Dan protested. "This shirt will be burned in a solemn ceremony just like Old Glory gets when she's tattered and soiled."

"You're mental."

"Never said I wasn't."

Skip veered off the road about two-hundred yards down the road and pulled his car behind a hedge-row that bordered a five acre field. He drove to a spot where the car was hidden behind the overgrown hedges and a group of pines. The car was well hidden from both the road, and the Stewart's farm. He shut off the engine.

The three men got out of the car and began scoping out the surrounding area.

Dan pointed at the hedges and shrubs. "Looks like these hedges and shit wrap all the way around this field," he said. "We should be able walk behind them and come up behind the barn without being seen."

Skip released the magazine on his 9mm. "Sounds like a plan," he said. He checked his ammo and slid the magazine back into the grip. He clicked it into place with a slap of his palm.

Red began walking along the hedge-row. "Let's rock and roll," he said.

"Let's rock and roll?" Dan asked.

"I knew I shouldn't have said it the second it rolled off my tongue," said Red.

"Then why did ya?"

"I thought it would sound cool." Red threw a thumb over his shoulder. "Skip always says, 'Sounds like a plan,' and he sounds cool."

"Thanks, Red Man," said Skip. "But remember, amigo, you ain't me."

It took the three men a little over twenty minutes to walk around the entire field and position themselves behind the red steel barn.

Dan peeked around the corner at the house. "Maybe we should have waited until night time," he said.

"I told ya," said Red.

Dan's eyes went to the Stewart's car, and then to a large wooden shed with a six foot over-head door. Next to the over-head door was a nine-lite steel entrance door. There were a number of other buildings on the property. Some looked as though they had once been garages for storing tractors and other farm machinery. Other buildings looked to be sheds for tools and equipment. The garages that were open were empty. The waitress had told them it was no longer a working farm, so Dan figured most of the equipment had probably been sold off over time. There were dirt roads and pathways that led from building to building. It was obvious that, in its day, the farm had been very well taken care of.

"You guys wait here for a second," Dan said. "I'm gonna see if I can get a little closer to the house."

Just as Dan started to walk around the barn, a man exited the house. Dan jumped back out of sight.

"What is it?" Red asked.

"Someone just came out of the house."

"Is it Lou?"

"No." Dan stealthily craned his neck around the corner post to get a better look. "I don't know who it is."

The tall muscular man climbed into the Stewart's Buick and drove down the dirt driveway. When he got to the road, he hung a left, and headed toward town.

"Change in plans," said Dan. "Come on, Skip."

"What about me?" Red asked.

"You wait here."

"Seriously?" Red protested. "I want to do something cool."

Dan shot Red a look over his shoulder. "Shut up," he said. "All the cool kids are waiting here."

"Very funny," Red replied.

Skip followed Dan around the barn and down the dirt path to the house. Dan quietly pulled open the screen door and tried the doorknob; it was unlocked. He pushed open the door with his fingertips. Dan froze at the loud creak of the door and waited for Lurch to say, "You rang?" It didn't happen.

"Buck?" a woman called out. "You forget something?"

Dan looked over his shoulder at Skip. "Yeah," he said in a deep voice, figuring that's how Buck would answer. He motioned for Skip to enter first, since he was the only one with a weapon.

Skip pulled the 9mm from his waistband and went in; Dan was right behind him.

They walked into a large kitchen. In the middle of the room was a long, rustic farmhouse table, stained a beautiful cherry finish, with a bench on each side. It reminded Dan of the Walton's dinner table. As a matter of fact, the entire kitchen brought back memories of Thursday nights as a kid watching the *The Waltons* with his sisters. There were wide plank floors and wallpaper on the walls. The ceiling was a beaded wainscoting that had been painted white. Everything looked original in the old farmhouse, and very well taken care of.

Skip crept over to a doorway on his left and looked into the living room.

"Buck?" the woman called out again.

Skip stepped into the opening. "Buck left," he said. "It's just us."

The woman was startled.

Dan moved up beside Skip. "Well, well," said Dan. "If it isn't the cigar-hating, dog shit complainer."

"What are *you* doing here?" asked Sandy.

"Looking for you," Dan answered. "And the Stewarts," he added. "Where do you have them? Tied up in a shed somewhere, I'm guessing."

"No," said Lou. "I'm right here."

Dan turned to see Lou holding a 12-gauge pump-action shotgun leveled at his belly. "Oh ... hey, Lou." he said.

"Drop that gun," said Lou.

Skip kept his gun on Sandy.

"Drop it or I'll cut him in half," Lou warned. "I never liked his smelly cigars and that goddamn dog either."

"Ouch," Dan said.

Skip gently placed the gun on the floor between him and Sandy.

"Pick it up, Sandy," Lou ordered.

Sandy bent down and grabbed it.

"Where's Alice?" Dan asked.

"She *is* tied up in a shed," Lou replied. He motioned toward the door with the shotgun. "You two idiots put your hands on top of your heads and start marching."

Dan and Skip complied. Once outside, Dan glanced over at the corner of the barn hoping Red was watching.

"Keep walking," Lou said. "Head to that shed over yonder."

Sandy walked along on their right with Skip's pistol pointed at them.

"Yonder?" Dan asked. "Is that left, or right."

"Shut up, smart ass."

"Did you kill Corky Maddigan?" Dan asked.

"Nope," Lou replied. "That moron got himself killed by someone else. Keep moving."

The shed was a red steel building, about 10x20. When they got to it, Sandy opened the door.

"Inside," said Lou.

Once Dan and Skip were inside the dark building Lou flipped on the light switch next to the door. Dan immediately saw Alice Stewart sitting near a support post. Her hands and feet were bound with baling twine, and a one-inch nylon rope was wrapped several times around her waist, tying her to the post. Dan had always thought her to be a nice-looking woman for her age, but in her current state, disheveled and distraught, she looked much older than her sixty-two years.

"Dan!" said Alice.

"Are you okay?" Dan asked.

Alice nodded her head yes.

Lou instructed Skip to tie Dan to another post—about eight feet away from Alice—in the same manner. When Skip finished, he stood and turned around. Lou slammed the butt of the shotgun into Skip's forehead. Skip crumpled to the ground, his head smacking the hard dirt floor. Blood ran from the gash where the shotgun hit him.

"Jesus Christ!" Dan shouted. He tried to free his hands, but Skip had done too good of a job. "You didn't have to do that, Lou!"

"You keep your mouth shut, Coast, or you'll get it next," Lou warned.

Sandy crouched down beside Skip. She put her palm on his chest. "I think you killed him, Lou."

"Tie him up," Lou said. "Just in case he's not dead yet."

Sandy dragged Skip across the floor by the leg to an eight foot wooden workbench. She bound his ankles together with the baling twine. She then rolled him over on his side and tied his wrists together. When she finished, Lou gave the ropes a couple yanks. When he was satisfied they would hold, he and Sandy left the building, turning off the light on his way out.

"Skip!" Dan called out. There was no movement from the young man. "Skip!" Dan kicked his feet at the small rocks and dirt, trying to rouse his friend. He closed his eyes for a few seconds, trying to adjust them to the darkness. He stared at Skip's back and shoulders looking for any encouraging signs of movement; there weren't any. He closed his eyes once again and opened them.

Two small skylights in the ceiling were so old and caked with dirt and grime that they let in almost no light. Dan could make out Skip's outline, but it was too dark to see if he was still breathing. "Dammit!" he said.

"I'm sorry, Dan," said Alice.

"Why didn't you warn me?" Dan asked.

"I couldn't," she explained. "Lou would only let me have my phone when someone called, and then he stood right next to me when I spoke. He told me what to say. He said he would kill me if I said the wrong thing. I didn't tell him you were with Red."

"So what the hell is going on, Alice. How long have you been tied up in here? Who killed Corky Maddigan? Was the dead guy at your house Forrest Franklin? Does this have anything to do with the bank rob—"

"Slow down, Dan, slow down," said Alice. "One thing at a time. Do the cops know you're here?"

"No."

"Does anyone know you're here?"

"Red is out there somewhere."

"Hopefully he went for help."

"Hopefully," said Dan. "Start from the beginning, Alice. What's going on here? Why is Lou doing this?"

Alice stared at the dirt floor. "Sandy is an old friend of Lou's. This was Lou's parents' farm."

"And the dead guy in your house in Key West?"

"That's Sandy's husband, Forrest. She told Lou that Forrest just collapsed the morning after they got there."

"The coroner said he had a heart attack."

"That's what Sandy figured."

"What about Corky Maddigan?"

"He was shot in his home."

"I know. By who?"

"No one knows."

"Who robbed the bank, Alice?"

"Lou, Nate, and Forrest."

"Nate?"

"Nate Grubbs. He's the caretaker here."

"Must be the big guy I saw leaving in your car earlier."

"Probably."

"Someone tried to kill us at our hotel last night, Alice. Was that Lou and Nate?"

"I didn't hear anything about it, but I would assume so. Lou was pretty angry when he found out you were here."

"Why were Sandy and Forrest at your house in Key West?"

"From what I overheard, everyone was supposed to meet there to split up the money."

"From what you heard?" Dan asked. "You weren't in on this whole thing?"

"Of course not!" said Alice indignantly. "How could you think I would be in on something like this?"

Dan gave her the old cocked eyebrow. "Well I have to say, Alice, I wouldn't have thought Lou would be in on a bank robbery either."

"There's things from Lou's past that most people don't know about."

"Swell. Let me guess: secret agent? Witness protection?"

"No, smartass, he just spent some time in prison when he was young … before he and I met."

"For what?"

"Driving the getaway car in a bank robbery."

"That's just great."

The door opened and Red stepped in front of the opening, blocking out the afternoon sun. "Dan," he whispered.

"Red! Thank God!" Alice whispered back "How'd you get in?" said Dan quietly.

"Easy, I saw where Sandy put the key."

"Good man."

"I just spoke to Chief Carver. He said he tried to call you."

"They took our cell phones," Dan explained.

Red stepped just inside the building. "Carver said that Lou Stewart was arrested once and spent time in prison for robbing a bank."

"No kidding," said Dan. "Untie me."

Red walked over and knelt down beside his friend.

"Are the cops on their way?" Dan asked.

"No. Why would they be?"

"Didn't you tell Rick what was going on here?"

"No."

"Why not, for Chrissakes?"

"I didn't know I was supposed to. You said you didn't want Rick to know we were here."

"That was before we were tied up in shed, and no one knew where we were."

"Oh, yeah," Red said, nodding his head. "I probably should have said something."

"Don't move!" came Lou Stewart's voice from the doorway.

"Shit!" swore Dan and Red in unison.

"Stand up, tubby" Lou ordered.

Red stood and turned around. "Don't shoot, Lou! It's me, Red Baxter."

"No shit." Lou motioned Red over to the workbench. "Sit over there."

Red looked down at Skip as he walked over. "Is he okay?" he asked.

"He's dead," said Lou, "and you will be too if you try anything stupid."

Red kept his eyes on Skip as he lowered himself to the floor and positioned his back up against the workbench.

"What's going on, Lou?" Nate Grubbs asked, as he stepped into the shed and flipped on the light switch. The room lit up and everyone squinted for a second. "Who the hell do we have here?"

Lou pointed the barrel of the gun at each of his prisoners. "That's Dan Coast. He's our drunken dip shit neighbor in Key West."

"Ouch," Dan said.

"That there's his retarded sidekick, Red Baxter."

"Wow," said Red.

"The dead guy there on the floor is some moron they call Skip."

"Didn't know there were three of ya," said Nate. "Only saw two men at the pool last night."

"I was doing somersaults in the pool," Red explained.

"Oh, were ya?" Nate mocked.

"These three idiots run around the Keys playing private investigator," said Lou.

Nate chuckled. "Not very good at their jobs, are they." He looked at Dan. "Did y'all solve the big case?" he teased.

Lou nodded his head at his wife. "I imagine she filled them in on everything."

Nate walked to Red and tied him securely to the other leg of the workbench. "What are we gonna do with 'em, Lou."

"Kill them, and bury them ... and not necessarily in that order."

Nate chuckled again. Dan thought for a bank robber, and possible murderer, Nate seemed like a pretty jovial guy.

Lou looked over at Alice. "You okay?"

"Am I okay?" she repeated. "I'm tied to a goddamn post in a goddamn shed."

"Are you thirsty, or hungry?"

"Like you give a shit."

"Sorry, Alice, but you just wouldn't listen. You gave me no choice. I can't go back to prison. I'm too old. I'd die in there." Lou turned and started for the door.

"You should have thought of that before you robbed a bank," Alice said.

Lou ignored her. He turned to Nate. "How'd things go in town?"

"Good," said Nate, "but you'll never guess what I heard at the diner."

"What's that?"

"That moron's cousin turned himself into the cops this morning."

Lou paused with his hand on the doorknob. "You mean Pete Maddigan?"

"Yep."

"Turned himself in for what?"

"Confessed to the cops that he shot Corky."

"Well, son of a bitch. I would have never guessed it." Lou took a deep breath and loudly sighed. "Did he turn in our money to the cops?"

"Don't know," Nate said. "All's I know is, he turned himself into the cops."

Lou paused for a moment in the doorway. He looked at Red and said, "Okay, tubby, let's have it."

"Have what?" said Red innocently.

"The key. I saw you pocket it. I shouldn't have been so careless with it, but we never expected company. Give it up."

Red shrugged. "Well, you can't blame a guy for trying. But you'll have to get the key yourself. I'm kinda … tried up here."

Frowning, Lou went to Red and dug his hand in the side pocket of the big man's shorts. "Watch out for the tube snake," Red warned.

Lou served him a wicked backhand slap with his free hand. "I've got it," he said. "Let's go."

Lou turned off the light and pulled the door closed. The captives heard the key engaging the lock. The sounds of their feet crunching against the crushed stone grew faint as they walked away from the building.

"So Pete killed Corky," Red said.

"Looks that way," said Dan.

"He seemed like a nice guy."

"So did Lou." Dan turned in Alice's direction. "What did Lou mean when he asked if Corky turned in their money?"

"Nate gave the money to Corky after the robbery, and told him to hang on to it for a few days," Alice responded. "They told him they would cut him in if he kept it at his place."

"Where's the getaway car?" asked Red.

"At the bottom of the pond out back," Alice said.

"Corky must have told Pete about the money," said Dan.

"But why would he kill him?" Red asked.

"Maybe Pete tried to take it," Dan answered. "Remember Pete's little spiel about him having to work for everything he had, but Corky never worked a day in his life? Maybe Pete figured this was just another one of those times, and he wanted his cut."

"Sounds good to me," said Red.

"Alice, how does Nate know Corky?" Dan asked.

"Everybody in town knows Corky," Alice replied. "He even helps Nate around the farm sometimes. They may have even gone to school together."

"Okay, let's see if I've got all this straight," said Dan musingly. "Lou, Forrest, and Nate rob a bank. Nate gives the money to Corky for safe keeping. Forrest and Sandy drive to the Stewarts' house in Key West to wait for everyone to join them. Corky tells his cousin Pete about the money. They fight over the money and Pete kills Corky. Forrest dies of a heart attack, and Sandy panics and returns to Bonifay alone."

"Looks like we solved another case," said Red.

"Solved a case!" Alice shouted. "I just sat here and told you the whole goddamn story."

"Yeah but—"

215

"Yeah but nothing," said Alice angrily.

Dan chuckled. "Whose idea was it to rob the bank, Alice?" asked Dan.

"Nate and Forrest," she answered. "Nate knew about Lou's past and asked him if he wanted in. They needed someone to drive the car."

"When did you find out about it?"

"Not until I got here on Saturday. Lou caught me eavesdropping on his and Nate's conversation. He tried to convince me to go along with them, but I said I wouldn't. That's when Lou tied me up in one of the bedrooms upstairs. He brought me out here Thursday night. He said I talked too much."

"Saturday?" Dan asked. "But the robbery was on Thursday. How did Lou drive the getaway car if you didn't get here until Saturday?"

"Lou took a flight back to Florida from Alaska two nights before the robbery. Lou told me there was an emergency here at the farm. Evidently they had been planning this robbery for over a year."

"So there really was an Alaskan cruise?"

"Yes," Alice said. "But I spent the last four days on it alone. I flew back here to meet with Lou after we docked the last time. I still can't believe he expected me to go along with it."

"And they've been planning it for a year. Seems like an awful lot of trouble and risk for eighty-thousand dollars."

"According to Nate and Forrest, there was supposed to be a lot more. There's this armored car that comes in the second Thursday of every month. There was supposed to be almost a million dollars in that bank. From what I overheard, the truck broke down on the way."

"Sounds like a lot of shit went wrong," Red said.

"You know, Alice," said Dan, "the only way out of this for them is to kill all of us and make a run for it."

"I know."

"And if Corky told Pete who robbed the bank, the cops will probably be here in a few hours."

"I have a date Friday night," Red said out of left field.

"Seriously?" Dan asked. "With who?"

"Char Walker, the sketch artist."

"No shit? I wondered about that."

"How come you never asked?"

"I didn't want to mention it, just in case she had shot you down."

"Well she didn't shoot me down. I asked her out, and she said yes."

"So, why are you bringing it up now?"

"Because I haven't had a date in over a year, and if I die today, I'm gonna be really pissed."

"Ohhhhh, aggggh," Skip moaned. "My head …"

"Skip!" Dan and Red cried in unison. "You're alive!"

Skip rolled onto his back. "What happened?"

Lou hit you in the head with the butt of his shotgun," said Dan.

"How long have I been out?"

"A few hours maybe."

"We thought you were dead," said Red.

"I think I was, dude. I remember seeing this light at the end of a long tunnel. My grammie was telling me—"

"They're going to kill us, Skip," Dan said.

"Oh, man!" Skip responded. "I can't die twice in one day. We gotta get out of here." Skip made a weak but valiant effort to stand and then realized his limbs were bound. "Whoa, dudes, someone tied me up."

"It was Lou," Dan informed him, "he knocked you out and had Sandy tie you up."

"What a dick, bro. Excuse my lingo, Mrs. Stewart."

"It's quite all right, Skip." Alice answered.

Skip wiggled his hands and tugged at his feet. "That Sandy chick must have been in the Girl Scouts." He stopped moving and stared straight ahead.

"Are you all right, Skip?' Red asked.

Skip said nothing.

"Skip?"

Skip's eyes rolled back in his head and he fell over, the side of his head smacking the hard dirt floor once again.

"He's out," Red said.

"We gotta get that boy to a doctor," said Alice.

"I wonder what time it is?" Dan said.

"Must be around one," Red responded. He leaned over as far as he could toward a thin separation in the steel siding. He tried to peer through the crack, but the light coming in was too bright.

"See anything?" Dan inquired.

"No."

The three prisoners sat there for what seemed like hours. Skip lay motionless eight feet away from Red. Their clothing was wet through from sweat.

"It's gotta be a hundred and ten degrees in here," Dan stated.

"At least," Red agreed.

Dan looked over at Alice; she was asleep, with her head against the support post. "She's gonna need water," he said.

"Me too," said Red.

A few more hours passed and the room darkened slightly. They could feel the temperature start to go down. The light coming from the crack in the steel wasn't as bright as before. They all looked at each other when they heard the sound of a vehicle approaching. The tires rolled across the crushed stone driveway.

"Can you see out there now?" Dan asked.

Red leaned over. "It's a cop car," he said.

"Thank God," said Alice. Her voice was raspy and her lips were dry. Her dehydrated body was no longer sweating.

The sound of the crunching stone ceased and the engine shut off. The car door opened.

"He's getting out of the car," Red said excitedly. "In here!" he shouted.

"We're in here!" hollered Alice.

"Hey!" Dan yelled.

"He heard us," Red said. "He heard us. In here!"

"In here!" Dan hollered. "We're being held prisoner! We've got an unconscious man in here, too!"

"They heard the officer try the door. "I'll have to shoot off the lock. Are you a safe distance from the entry?"

"Wait!" said Dan. "You'll tip them off."

But it was too late. They heard a loud bang. The shed door opened and dim evening light filled the room. A young police officer stood in the doorway. Smoke curled from the barrel of the revolver in his hand. "What's going on in here?" he asked.

"We need help," Dan said. "They tied us up."

"They're the ones who robbed the bank," Red added.

"Untie us," said Alice. "Quick before they come back!"

"Slow down," said the young officer. "One at a time."

"There's two men in the house," Dan explained. "They're the ones who robbed the bank. They tied us—"

The sound of Lou's shotgun was deafening. The three on the floor watched as the officer's chest tore open, sending blood, bone, and organ flying into the room. His lifeless body was catapulted forward, following the bloody cloud. He hit the dirt floor inches from Alice's feet.

Alice screamed. Her face and clothing were covered in blood. Alice continued to scream hysterically.

Lou stepped into the shed, closed the door behind him, and flipped on the light. His eyes went from Alice to Dan, and then to Red as he pumped the shotgun. "This is on all y'all. You lured that poor kid in here."

Alice didn't let up. "Why? Why?" she screamed.

"Shut up!" Lou hollered.

"Don't do this, Lou," said Dan.

Lou side stepped over in front of Red and Skip. He raised the shotgun and pointed it at Dan. Dan closed his eyes, gritted his teeth, and waited for the shot.

Skip had come to some minutes before but had been playing 'possum. Now he rolled to his side, and with his bound ankles, swept Lou's legs out from underneath him. Lou hit the dirt on his ass, firing the shotgun through the ceiling.

Skip rolled onto his back and pushed against the ground with his shoulders, lifting his legs in the air, positioning Lou's neck between his knees. He squeezed his legs together choking Lou.

Lou dropped the shotgun and struggled to free himself. Skip applied more pressure, twisted at the hip, and with one quick jerk, snapped Lou's neck like a twig.

Lou's lifeless body slumped and fell backwards. Skip released his grip and squirmed to get his legs out from under Lou.

Dan slowly opened his eyes, surprised he was still alive. "Holy crap," he said.

"Can you see the front door of the house through that crack?" Skip asked.

Red returned his attention to the seam in the steel siding. "Yes," he said. "I can see it."

"Let us know if anyone comes out side."

Skip, being the only one not tied to anything, stood and started a search for anything with a sharp edge. He quickly spotted an old scythe hanging on the wall. He hopped over and with his hands on opposite sides of the blade, rubbed the baling twine back and forth against the blade until the twine fell from his hands. He bent down and removed the twine from his ankles.

"Untie me," Dan said.

"Wait! Someone's coming," said Red.

Skip grabbed Lou's rifle and pumped the stock with one hand. He pointed the weapon at the door and waited.

"It's Nate," Red said.

Everyone remained silent as they listened for the crunching of stone. As the sound grew closer, Skip readied himself.

The door opened. No one was there.

Suddenly Nate leapt from behind the door into the opening, his 9mm in his two-fisted grip. His finger twitched on the trigger.

Skip fired the shotgun, hitting Nate in the belly and sending him sailing backwards through the air. The stone made one final crunch as Nate's body landed.

"Like shootin' fish in a barrel," Skip commented coldly.

"Pat yourself on the back later," said Dan. "Now untie us so we can get the hell out of here."

When Dan, Red, Skip, and Alice quietly entered the old farmhouse, Sandy was sitting on the couch in the living room, with her back to the doorway. She was watching the local news.

Alice looked over at the thick handle of the old corn husk broom leaning against the wall.

"Find out what all the commotion was, Nate" said Sandy casually. She continued to stare at the television.

"The cops aren't saying anything about Pete Maddigan turning in the money. So either he didn't turn it in, or they're not releasing that information. They haven't even mentioned the bank robbery, so we might still be in the clear."

"Mmm-hmm," said Dan, trying once again to sound like Nate.

"I only heard three shots out there," said Sandy. "Who's still alive?"

"Just you," said Alice.

Sandy spun around just in time to see the handle of the broom coming at her. Her eyes grew to twice their size, but only for a split second. The handle hit her in the side of the head and she was out cold.

All three men cringed at the sickening sound of wood against skull.

"Ouch," Dan said. "Heard that same sound once at a Yankees game. An old lady got hit right in the bean with a foul ball. Sounded just like that."

Alice stared over the back of the couch at Sandy's unconscious body. "Bitch," she said.

Chapter Twenty-Six

Dan told Skip to wait about ten minutes before calling the cops, then he and Red ran back to Skip's car, and headed back toward town.

"Why did you tell Skip to wait awhile before calling the police?" Red asked.

"Because I wanted to get away from the farm before they showed up," Dan answered. "I didn't want to hang around there all night answering questions."

"Oh. Where are we going?"

Dan sighed. "Back to the blind guy's house."

"I knew it!" Red shouted.

As Dan steered the car around the bend where County Road 173 turns into East North Avenue, four cop cars flew by them with their light bars flashing and their sirens wailing.

"Must be some trouble somewhere," Dan joked.

"Looks that way," said Red. "So ya think the blind guy was in on it? I told ya I didn't trust blind people."

"Oh shut up." Dan turned left onto Waukesha Street. "How the Christ do I get back over to McGee Street?" He read each street sign as they passed.

"I think if you take a right up here," Red said, pointing down the street.

"Veterans Boulevard," Dan read aloud. "That doesn't sound familiar.'

"Because we're coming from the other direction."

"Should I turn here?"

"Yes!" Red shouted. "Jeez, it's like riding somewhere with my mother."

"Yeah, well, when I'm riding your mother—"

"Shut up."

Dan took the right onto Veterans Boulevard and then a left on McGee Street.

"Told ya," said Red.

"Told ya," Dan aped.

Dan pulled the car to the side of the street and parked in front of the old blind guy's house. He shut off the engine and the two men got out of the car. They stood in the old man's yard and looked at the two cop cars parked at Corky Maddigan's house. There was also a coroner's van in Corky's driveway. A cop outside glanced over and Dan waved. The cop waved back.

"Should we surround the place?" Red asked.

"Let's just knock on the door," Dan replied.

Dan rapped on the door a few times and they waited. The door opened and there stood the blind guy wearing his sunglasses and leaning on his cane.

"Good afternoon," Dan said.

"Dan Coast, and his associate, Red Baxter," said the old guy.

"You remembered."

"Yep."

"Just from hearing our voices," said Red. "That's pretty amazing."

"Yep."

"We never got your name, sir," said Dan.

"Bernerd Boothe."

"Can we come in, Bernerd?" Dan asked.

"What fer?"

"Just to talk."

"About what?"

"Corky Maddigan."

"Detective was here earlier. He said Corky had been killed."

"We know."

"They say his cousin killed him during an argument."

"That's what we heard."

"So then, what's there to talk about?"

"The money," said Dan.

"What money's that?" asked Bernerd.

"I see your house is for sale, and the other day when we knocked, you asked if we were from the bank."

"So?"

"Were you expecting someone from the bank?" asked Red.

"Maybe I was."

"They're foreclosing on you, aren't they?" Dan said.

"Yep. Been tryin' to sell the place for almost a year. Market around here ain't what it used to be."

"How far are you behind?" Dan asked.

"Six months. Ain't paid the taxes in a year. They want me outta here by the end of next week, but I ain't got nowhere to go. Had the place paid off once, but after the wife died I lost my health insurance. Before the Medicare kicked in I was paying out of pocket for everything. Got so far behind I had to take out a new mortgage."

"How far are you behind money-wise?" Dan pressed.

The old man hung his head. "A little over forty-grand."

"And that's why Corky gave you the money. He figured you could pay off everything you owed and get ya all caught up. Then you could stay. You're the only real friend Corky ever had."

"Most people took advantage of that boy," said Bernerd. "I couldn't believe it when he told me those assholes talked him into holding that money for them."

"You know you can't keep that money," said Dan.

"Yeah, I knew it when he gave it to me. But there was a part of me that thought, *fuck that bank.*"

Dan smiled. "I know what you mean."

228

Bernerd turned around. "I'll get you that money."

"Wow, that sucks," Red whispered.

"Yeah," Dan agreed. "It sure does."

"I feel like we should let him keep the money."

"It's not our decision to make. Besides, in the next few days, if not hours, Pete Maddigan is going to admit that he killed Corky in an argument over the money. *And* the Peoples South Bank is going to wonder how Bernerd Boothe came up with forty grand a few weeks after their bank was robbed."

"I guess you're right," Red admitted.

"Usually," said Dan.

Bernerd returned to the door holding a small black duffle bag. He held it out in front of him. "It's all in there," he said. "Just tell them I'm blind and didn't know what was in there."

Dan chuckled. "That was the plan."

Dan took the bag, and he and Red walked across the front yards to Corky's house.

"Excuse me," said Dan. "I think you might be looking for this."

The officer he waved to earlier cocked his head. "What is it?"

"A little over eighty grand." Dan jiggled the bag. "And some odd change."

Chapter Twenty-Seven

Two days later, back in Key West, Dan and Red got their asses chewed out by Chief Rick Carver. This was a common occurrence, but this time it was a little different. Rick yelled a lot, but his face never turned red, and he never once threatened to shoot either one of them. He never once called Dan a drunken moron, or called Red an idiot. At one point there may have even been a "great job" thrown in. Dan and Red both knew this was a mystery they would have to solve.

Alice Stewart hadn't returned to her home in Key West yet, but Dan had spoken to her a few times over the phone since the incident. She told Dan that according to the district attorney, there would probably be no charges brought against her. They had no reason not to believe her story.

Skip was still in the hospital. He spent one night in Doctor's Memorial in Bonifay, and was then moved by ambulance to the Lower Keys Medical Center.

This afternoon, after Rick's ass-chewing, Dan stood in line at the Centennial Bank in Key West. "I can help the next person in line," said the female teller, a young redhead.

Dan pulled his driver's license out of his money clip and placed it on the counter. "I need a cashier's check made out to Mr. Bernerd Boothe in the amount of forty-five thousand dollars."

The teller waved over an older woman who was sitting behind a desk. "It's my first day," she confided to Dan.

"Wow, you look much older," Dan joked. She didn't get it.

After leaving the bank, Dan stopped at the Fed-Ex Center at the end of Stickney Lane, and had the cashier's check overnighted to Bernerd. Bernerd would never know where the money came from. Well, he might put two and two together and realize Dan was the benefactor, but Bernard wasn't dumb. Blind, but not dumb. He'd never acknowledge Dan's generosity. And that's just how Dan wanted it.

A silver Ford F-150 with side rail toolboxes and a ladder rack was parked in Dan's driveway when he got home from FedExing the check. Dan parked his Porsche in the street. Rick's guy, Colton Masters, was working on the new picture window. *What the Christ?* Was Dan's first thought upon first seeing the shirtless young man on the step ladder. He was about thirty years old and gorgeous.

Maxine was sweeping the hardwood floor when Dan entered the house. She turned her head from the window when she heard the door open, and returned her attention to the floor.

"He's doing a pretty good job," Dan said.

"Is he?" Maxine asked. "I haven't really been paying much attention."

"Really Maxine? I'm not gay and I can't stop staring at him."

"Meh. He's not really my type."

"Okay." Dan looked up at the hole in the ceiling. "He say anything about that?"

"He said he'll start on that tomorrow."

Dan's eyes went to the painting between the windows behind the couch, and then to the painting on the wall across from it. They were both beach scenes. One was a sunset painted from Mallory Square, and the other was a full moon reflected on the water. "You haven't told me yet, how much were those?"

"Twelve-hundred each."

"Good God."

"Stacey's a talented artist."

"She's no Bob Ross. Where's the dog?"

"He was lying on Bev's deck the last I saw him."

Dan went to the bar and made himself a tequila, Seven, and lime. "You want a drink?" he asked.

"No, thanks," said Maxine.

Dan grabbed the morning's edition of the Key West Citizen and walked out the back door. Buddy lifted his head at the sound of the screen door's creak.

"Come on, boy!" Dan called out.

Buddy just dropped his head back to the deck and closed his eyes.

"Asshole," mumbled Dan. He walked down the gravel path to the two Adirondack chairs by the fire pit and sat down. He took a sip of his drink and set it on the ground next to his chair. He pulled out his cell phone and Googled *The Amazing Gary*. He put Gary's number in his contacts. Just as he was placing the cell phone back in his pocket, it rang. Dan looked at the caller ID, wondering who it was; the screen read UNKNOWN NUMBER.

"Hello?" said Dan.

"Dan? Dan Coast?" It was a female voice, young.

"Right both times."

"It's Maggie—Maggie Harrison."

"Doesn't ring a bell."

"From the State Motel in Haines City."

"Oh, yeah. You said your name was Marilyn Martin at the time."

"Yes."

"What can I do for you, Maggie?"

"It's my father, Mr. Coast. He killed my mother and blamed it on my boyfriend. And now I think he's trying to kill me. Mr. Coast, you said if I ever needed anything, I just had to call."

"What the Christ?"

The End

Coming Soon:

From the Tales of Dan Coast

Another Mother

Sunrise City Series
Sunrise City
Sunrise City 2: From Bad to Worse
Never Strikes Twice

Fernandina Beach Mysteries

Maintenance Required
High Maintenance

From Here to There: A Collection of Short Stories